PRICKLE POD HERO

GLENDA RICHMOND SLATER

Point Clear, Alabama

Published by:
www.IntellectPublishing.com

Prickle Pod Hero

Cover Illustration by David Philips
Book and Cover Design by Jessica Trippe

Hardback ISBN: 978-1-954693-20-3
Paperback ISBN: 978-1-954693-21-0

PRICKLE POD HERO

CHAPTER ONE

UNDER THE PORCH

"You two get on outta here," Pap yells. "Go see your pal Rick. Go climb your old magnolia tree. Find yourselves some place cool—October the first and it's still hotter'n a blast furnace."

Billy and Punchy start down the porch steps just as Pap starts up them. Punchy bumps into Pap's leg and Pap's heavy work boot shoots out and glances off the little dog's rump. Punchy yelps and runs under the porch. From the way he runs it looks like he's not hurt, but Billy gives his grandpap a look.

This is the worst Pap's been since Grandmam died. He's been drinking already and it's not even two o'clock. He can't sit still. For the past half hour he's been coming outside every few minutes, looking up the gravel road. Usually on Saturdays they go to the grocery store, but when Billy asked about that, Pap said they didn't need anything.

Billy opened cans of Vienna Sausage and got out Cheerios and milk for their breakfast. Then he and Punchy stayed outside until lunch, which was peanut butter and honey sandwiches and more milk. Not much for an almost 13-year-old, but he was more interested in staying out of Pap's way than in looking for more food. His grandpap hadn't eaten much of anything. After lunch, Billy sat on the swing and read his Superman comic books while Punchy sniffed around for lizards and toads.

Now Pap crosses the porch and opens the screen door. Without looking at Billy he says, "You heard me, Billy Boy. You and Punchy go on," and he goes inside. Billy whistles. Punchy's head appears from under the porch. He looks for Pap, then comes out and the two run down the road. They stop as soon as they round the bend and are hidden by the blackberry bushes growing along the barbed wire fence.

"Pap acts like he's expecting somebody, Punch," Billy says. "And he sure don't want us around. Well, I reckon we're not leaving 'til I find out what's going on."

He takes a peek. No sign of Pap. They walk back quietly and crawl under the porch. The dirt feels cool on the scorching hot day. "Quiet, Punchy," Billy says. While they wait, Billy rubs the thin brown leather band on his left wrist. Sure enough, in about ten minutes a pickup truck with two men in it rattles down the gravel road, turns onto the dirt driveway and parks behind Pap's old car. Billy hopes it's somebody who'll get his grandpap to settle down.

Pap's been worried for the past couple of weeks. Billy figures it has to do with money, but he knows better than to ask a lot of questions. His grandpap's hard to live with when he's upset. Not as hard as Billy's mama was though. It's easier to live with just Pap than when she was there, too. Seemed like she was always upset about something.

Two strange men get out of the rusty pickup. It looks like about a 1939 Ford. That would make it ten years old. Looks like it's not been treated too good. The guys stretch and scratch and look around, then come on up the steps and tromp across the porch. Billy crawls over and peers up at them through a crack as they stand at the front door. The driver has a big belly hanging over his belt and greasy hair with streaks of gray in it sticking out from under a dirty brown cowboy hat. The other one's a good bit younger, but no cleaner. Billy thinks he may have seen him before, but there's so many skinny, dark-haired guys with pimply faces and baseball caps riding around in pickup trucks and they're all pretty much alike. Except this one has more pimples than most.

The young one bangs on the screen door and Pap yells, "Come on in."

Billy notices they don't bother to wipe their boots and those boots could stand a good cleaning. They must have come straight from a cow pasture. The smell is strong all the way down to Billy's hideaway. He knows they're leaving tracks.

"Mighty hot drive all the way down here." The older man has a gravelly voice. "It looks like fall ain't never gonna come. Makes a fellow mighty thirsty."

"I'll get you some water," Billy hears his grandpap say. "Or I got some whiskey. You rather have that?" Billy's surprised at the offer, but not surprised when Fat Man and Pimples take Pap up on it. Pap's footsteps go over to the corner cupboard.

The threadbare sofa squeaks as the visitors sit down. The little wood house is built on a concrete foundation, so Billy can't get under the front room. He gets close as he can and lies on his back, still as a possum, with his hands cupping his ears and Punchy close up to him, quiet as Billy.

Nothing's being said. Billy hears the corner cupboard door open and close, then he figures Pap's gone to the kitchen for glasses. He pictures him standing at the kitchen table, pouring about an inch of whiskey in each glass. He knows it won't be any more than that for visitors. In a few minutes, Pap's big old green chair squishes as he sits down.

It's quiet for a bit, then Pap starts talking. Fast and not very loud. Billy can only get snatches of what he's saying. Something about a job. Something about land. Something about the government. Then the other two chime in and it's hard to make sense of any of it with three talking at once.

Billy hears Pap say "fifty dollars" real plain. There's an argument after that, with "not enough" shouted a few times and Pap getting louder and louder about it being "plenty for an easy job," and finally, in a quieter voice that Billy knows means business: "Well, take it or leave it. There's other folks'll do it for less."

The guys must know Pap means what he says, because they decide to take it. Fat Man gravels out an "Okay" and Pimples whines, "It ain't enough, but I guess I'm in."

"All right then, here's what you're gonna do," says Pap. His voice drops lower and the other two sit there *uh huh-ing* and *all-righting* and *we can do that-ing*.

The green chair squishes again as Pap pushes up out of it and says in his regular voice, "You get on it Monday night. It sure ain't gonna rain and there won't be anybody driving around down there then. Fifty dollars cash money when it's done, and not a word about this to anybody. You got that?"

"We got it," Fat Man says. "Now, how's about a little more of that whiskey? Seal the deal."

"Naw," says Pap. "No more drinking 'til you finish the job. That's an order. You're gonna need clear heads and steady hands. Now listen here, you go on now to see it, but just drive by. I don't want you stopping there. Sometimes there's kids around. Drive by it to get the lay of the land. No stopping in town, neither. You'd be noticed. Just haul yourselves on up the road—you got a ways to go."

The two guys clomp over to the front door and come out onto the porch. Billy scoots back to the crack. They don't look too happy. They go straight down the steps, get in the pickup, back out of the dirt drive and take off the way they came, with tires squealing and throwing up gravel. Like Fat Man's getting in the last word.

Pap comes out and watches the truck drive up the road. Then he goes back inside. Billy hears his footsteps heading for the kitchen. He thinks he knows what Pap's going for: more whiskey.

Billy wishes he could go talk to Rick, but he knows Rick's not home. Oh well, that's okay. "Come on, Punchy," he whispers. And the two of them set off at a run, headed for Lost Lane.

CHAPTER TWO

LOST LANE

Billy and Punchy run until they round the bend in the road.
"Boy howdy, it *is* hot as a blast furnace, Punchy." Billy stops and unbuttons his shirt, flapping it to stir up some air on his chest. Punchy shakes himself. Dirt from under the porch flies out of his brown coat. Billy bends over and brushes dirt out of his brown hair.

They cross to the woods on the right side of the road. It's just a little way to where the wax myrtle bushes start. They're big and thick, with weeds and ivy and dead leaves hiding the bottom of the row, and dense woods behind them. Billy goes through the tall weeds. He gets down and crawls through a small hole at the bottom of the bushes, into the world of the big oaks. Punchy is right behind him. Billy stops and takes a deep breath. For just a moment he forgets his worries. Punchy sniffs his way deeper into the woods. When Billy catches up, the little mutt is at Lost Lane, waiting for him.

Now they're free. Hidden from everything and everybody except birds and critters and bugs. Punchy doesn't bark in Lost Lane. He's been trained not to announce their special place to anybody that might be in earshot. But Billy says "Quiet, Punch" anyway, then lifts his arms and runs, holding his shirt so it balloons out behind him. Punchy zig-zags ahead.

The tall live oaks reach out for each other to make a tangled green roof high over the narrow path. Today they are very still.

Halfway along the lane, Billy sits down and Punchy comes back and jumps into his arms, licking his face, wagging his stumpy tail.

"You're a good boy," says Billy. He pats the scruffy head and kisses the little square muzzle, then lays back on the path. Punchy flops down beside him, panting. Billy feels the little dog's rump to make sure it's not sore from Pap's boot. Punchy doesn't show any reaction. Billy pats him again.

"Pap didn't mean it, Punch. He's nervous," he says. And thinks to himself: *Yeah, and he's drinking. He's bad about that ever since Grandmam died. But this ain't about Grandmam. It's something else.* He keeps thinking about Pap and Fat Man and Pimples and what he's heard from under the porch. He rubs the leather band on his wrist and feels the letters burned into it: WAB. Finally, the bad thoughts began to slip away, he gets quiet and he and Punchy start to drift off to sleep.

Loud voices and truck doors slamming jar them awake. Then a motor starts. It sounds like it's down close to the Tree.

"Hey! It's that old pickup," Billy whispers. "It made that grinding noise when it started at the house. Come on, Punchy."

They run to where the lane ends and squeeze between dense trees and vines into thick laurel bushes. Billy stands on tiptoe and eases his head up just in time to see the pickup drive onto the paved county road. As soon as it's out of sight he and Punchy push through the laurels and run for the Tree.

"That was the truck, all right. And look at those tracks—those guys drove right up here under the Tree." *What are they doing down here,* he wonders. *Does this have something to do with what Pap's hiring them for?*

Billy walks all around the huge magnolia tree. His Tree. It looks just the same. The big limb is leaning down almost to the ground, like always. He walks on it to the trunk and climbs halfway up to check the hidey hole. Slingshot and shells and arrowheads still there. Only thing different is suddenly he feels a strong stream of cool air coming from above. He looks up. It feels good on his sweaty face. But how can there be such a cool spot in the Tree on a day this hot? Now the stream moves over to his shoulder. Feels like somebody's pointing a fan at him. Can't be anybody up there, but he calls out anyway, "Hey! What's going on?" Punchy starts barking. Billy looks down through the thick leaves. He can see the little dog standing on the low limb, looking up into the Tree. Making a real fuss. The cool air stops.

Billy shakes his head. Nothing there, just a weird bit of breeze. Maybe stirred up by the Tree, just for him. Could be, but he wouldn't ever tell anybody else he thought so. He could have told Grandmam. She'd have said the Tree could do that.

"Okay, Punchy, you're right. We better get on home." As he climbs down, a picture of Fat Man and Pimples standing on Pap's front porch flashes into his mind. If Pap is involved in some kind of a deal with those two...well, it's not likely to be anything good. It looks like Pap was telling them to go see the Tree. And telling them not to stop there. If so, they sure ignored that order. What about Pap saying come back on Monday night? They might ignore him on that, too, and come back sooner. But come back for what? Billy gets a sick feeling in the pit of his stomach. He doesn't want to leave his Tree.

Punchy doesn't want to leave the Tree, either, but it's because he knows there's something up there—*something different*. He keeps barking at it, even when Billy picks him up and carries him, but once they're in Lost Lane he gets quiet, Billy puts him down, and the two run fast as they can.

Billy's mind is on Pap and that truck. He forgets about the cool air in the Tree. Punchy, though, remembers the *something*. What he doesn't know is that it's following him and Billy home.

CHAPTER THREE

AT THE TOP OF THE TREE

The *something different* detected by Punchy is Autumn 1949. She had arrived late the night before: Friday, September 30, according to her All-Seasons Calendar. East Wind flew her down and they had made good time.

Autumn isn't sure exactly where she has arrived to, but she thinks it must be the Deep South because it is steaming hot. She can't consult her Nature Atlas. It fell out of her cape pocket as they blew along and East Wind said he didn't have time to back up to find it; he had an appointment on the East Coast the next day and didn't want to be late for it. So they'd continued on, too high up to see much even while old Sol was still making his way across the sky and there was plenty of light.

It was very dark when, without any warning whatsoever, East Wind dropped her off. He was up and away before she could thank him or ask where she was. She did know that she was on a tree top. She had landed softly, even though the leaves were big and stiff. As she came down, they gave way to her shape and enfolded her in a hug and she heard the tree give a little sigh. She had felt quite welcomed.

But Autumn 1949 is worried. She knows she hasn't had enough training. She was in the Weatherlings program only two months, following Mother Nature around, trying to take it all in. Mama N, as her apprentices called her, wouldn't slow down and seldom seemed to hear Autumn's questions, let alone answer them. There had been a shortage of apprentices and she had taken Autumn on, even though she said Autumn didn't show much promise as a Weatherling.

"You seem to tire easily," Mama N had said. "And you're too curious about everything. You get side-tracked. You need to learn to keep your mind on the job. Focus, girl, *focus*."

They were Up North in Minnesota when Winter blew in, saying a Weatherling had to get down to the Deep South and get things started. He'd heard from West Wind that whoever had been sent there had blown it. Winter thought that was funny and repeated *blown it*, but Mama N didn't smile. Anyway, he said, it was late September and Summer was still hanging around.

Winter was a big talker. "I stay away from the Deep South for the most part because people there don't like me. I've never felt welcome. And I've heard through the Weathervine that people are saying it's hotter than a blast furnace down there right now."

Mama N had narrowed her eyes at him and started tapping her long, brown fingers, so he said he'd better get on back to Canada, and he skydoodled. A big whoosh, and a frigid blast down Autumn's back, and he was out of there.

Mama N turned her dark brown eyes on Autumn. "You! Autumn 1950! Where's Autumn 1949?

"I beg your pardon, Ma'am, but I am Autumn 1949."

"Oh, for the love of Sol! All this time I thought I was training Autumn 1950. If you're Autumn 1949, you aren't supposed to be here. No wonder things are fouled up down there in...where did he say?"

Autumn knew this was a test. "He said the Deep South, Ma'am, but I don't know where it is." She hesitated before going on. "And I think I may need more training."

"More training, Weatherling?" Mama N's brown eyes turned to emerald green and little lightning flashes darted around in them.

"I've been training you for months, you nature ninny. Now get yourself down there. Immediately! On the double! Pronto!"

Pronto? That was a new one, but Autumn got the idea.

"Yes Ma'am. How...how do I get there?"

"The usual way, you simple seedling. Now skydoodle!" barked Mama N. She blinked her now purple eyes twice and was gone.

East Wind came along just then and offered Autumn a ride, so she wrapped her filmy orange-streaked cape around her long, thin body and they were off before she could say Jumping Jack Frost.

Now here she is in the Deep South. She guesses. She knows she should get started on her job. But it's too dark and her tree bed feels so good. She blows a little pillow of cool air and lies there, thinking. It definitely is extremely hot. Hot as a blast furnace, Winter had said. How hot does a blast furnace get? As for that matter, what is a blast furnace? That must be in Weatherling Summer's bailiwick. Which brings up the question, how is she going to find Summer and tell her to get out of the Deep South and head Up North and report in to Mama N? Maybe Summer would be exhausted with hanging around so long in a place as hot as a blast furnace. Or...what if she liked blast furnaces and decided not to leave? And, even if she left, would Autumn know what to do to get the new Season going?

All these worries. All that skydoodling. All this heat. All the things she doesn't know. She snuggles into the big welcoming leaves and the next thing she doesn't know is that she has fallen asleep.

Late afternoon of the next day, she's awakened by the sound of someone climbing the tree. She checks her All-Seasons Calendar. Good heavens, it's Saturday, October first and Sol is well over west in the sky. She slides down a little way. It's a very big tree. She goes down farther to see what's happening. There's a boy reaching into a hole in the tree trunk. He looks so sweaty and red-faced she can't resist downstretching and blowing some cool air on him. He looks up, startled. Below, a dog starts barking. The boy calls out—calls the dog Punchy—then begins to climb down. But he keeps looking back.

Autumn, of course, is curious. When the boy and dog leave they squeeze through thick bushes onto a path through big trees. She follows them, staying at the top of the trees and a little behind, where the boy can't feel the cool air she's letting out in small puffs, and the dog can't detect the scent of fall that clings to her cape.

CHAPTER FOUR

SUPPERTIME

Billy and Punchy come up the dirt driveway quietly. Billy wants to see what kind of mood Pap's in before they go inside. He doesn't hear anything. Maybe Grandpap is asleep in his big chair. But when they get to the steps they smell bacon. Pap must be cooking supper. A good sign. Boy, it smells good.

Before they go onto the porch Billy brushes himself off again and buttons his shirt. He tries to smooth down his hair. It's still pretty dirty and standing up even worse than usual. Well, at least the brown dirt's about the same color as his hair and his shirt. His dungarees are always dirty, anyway. He kneels down to pull some cockleburs off his pants and off of Punchy. The little dog backs away and shakes himself.

"Sorry, Punch," Billy says.

Punchy's water bowl is empty. Billy dips water from the bucket on the porch rail to rinse out the bowl, then fills it to rinse his own sweaty face and dirty hands. He throws that water out and puts in some more and while Punchy has a drink, Billy gets himself a dipperful. Then he opens the screen door and calls out, "Hey, Pap, we're back."

"Hey, Billy Boy. I was about to get worried about you two." Sure enough, Pap is in the kitchen. "Come on in here and help me with these eggs. It's bacon and eggs and biscuits tonight. How's that sound? You didn't get much of a breakfast this morning."

"Sounds good, Pap. Smells good, too." Pap isn't scolding and he's cooking supper, so Pap's not mad. There aren't any tracks on the porch or in the living room. Pap must've cleaned up after those dirty boots. That's another good sign.

Punchy lingers by the door while Billy goes over to the stove. Pap looks at the dog, picks up a piece of bacon from the stack he's already fried, and throws it over to him. Punchy catches it and gulps it down.

"What've you and Punchy been up to all this time?" Pap darts looks at Billy out of the corner of his eye, all the while turning bacon slices in the skillet with a long fork.

"Aw, you know. Pretty much what we always do. Messed around awhile in the woods. Laid down and cooled off for a while. Went down to the magnolia. Looks like somebody drove right up to it. They drove over bushes and everything."

As he talks, Billy breaks eggs into a bowl. He doesn't look at Pap.

"Is that right?" Pap asks. "Well, Saturdays people drive around, I reckon. Maybe they just wanted to get a good look at that big old tree. You actually see anybody?" He's thinking, *Dang those two, I told 'em not to stop down there.*

"Naw, didn't see nobody." That was true—he'd seen the truck but didn't actually see who was in it. "Pap, you really making biscuits? You ain't done that in a month of Sundays. A month of Saturdays, neither." Billy laughs good and loud, trying to get Pap's mind on something else, at least for the moment. He knows that sooner or later he's going to have to ask Pap about those guys. His stomach knots up at the thought.

Pap grins. "Yeah, I thought maybe you'd like a change." He throws another piece of bacon to Punchy. Billy figures he's saying sorry for being mean that morning. He figures Punchy knows it, too.

"That bacon sure looks good, Pap. Can I have a piece or is Punchy going to get it all?" Pap throws a slice to Billy and he catches it and Pap laughs.

After supper, Punchy goes outside while Billy and Pap wash and dry the dishes and then head for the front room. Billy turns on the radio. They settle down to listen to the adventures of *The Shadow* and *Mr. Chameleon*, two of their favorite programs. An hour later, after Mr. Chameleon solves his case, Pap gets up.

"Okay, Billy Boy, time to hit the hay," he says. He goes to the door and calls Punchy in.

Billy isn't sleepy. He's thinking again about those two guys. But he goes into his bedroom and Punchy follows to settle down on the ragged blue blanket next to the bed. Pap switches the radio dial to country music. Listening to Eddy Arnold sing, and rubbing on his wristband, helps calm Billy. When his grandpap peeks into the bedroom later, Billy and Punchy are asleep.

Pap goes to the front door and looks out into the dark. He shakes his head. "Stupid. Drove right up to it after I told 'em just drive by. Stupid, or just plain ornery. Probably both. Well, I guess I'm stuck with 'em now."

CHAPTER FIVE

AUTUMN AND THE TREE

Autumn watches from the top of a tall pine tree as the boy and dog go into the house. It's small and the rough wood siding could use a coat of paint, but it has a porch across the front that looks awfully inviting. She slides halfway down the tree and floats over onto it. She hears the boy call out "Hey Pap, we're back," as he goes through the door and a voice answers from the back of the house. She whooshes herself over the house and sees a smaller porch there and a door to the kitchen. She peeks in. A man is at the stove, cooking. That must be Pap. He's very skinny and looks old, but moves around fast. He's asking the boy questions. Billy Boy, he calls him.

Autumn is all set to settle down by the door and hear what the boy has to say, but Mama N's words come back to her: *You're too curious. You have to learn to stay focused on what you're supposed to be doing.*

Mama N was right. Autumn's so interested in the boy and the dog that she's forgotten all about her mission: to get Summer to clear out. Of course, her first task is to *find* Summer. But she hopes she'll see Billy Boy and Punchy again. She takes off fast, whooshing herself up above the treetops until she gets to the little hidden lane. She can't resist gliding down and walking the rest of the way to her Tree.

It's getting dark, but not too dark to get a good look at the Tree. Autumn outstretches her arms and encircles the grey-brown trunk. She has never come across such a big tree! She pulls her arms back in and moves around it slowly, sliding her long hands on the rough bark and getting pleasant, tingly sensations. It is, for sure, a friendly tree. She floats up into it. The leaves are long, thick, pointed. They're shiny, waxy, dark green on top, with rusty-red bottoms that feel fuzzy to her fingertips. The shape sort of reminds her of a canoe she and Mama N once saw on a lake in Minnesota. The tree is covered with leaves and there are plenty of them on the ground, too. Most of the fallen ones have turned brown.

Autumn sees hard, brown, cone-shaped pods on the ground and on the tree. They have a tough little twig-stick that attaches to the branches and they are full of cavities holding bright red seeds. Little tough points stick up all over. The pods on the ground have lost their seeds, but not their prickly points.

Autumn starts climbing higher. It's quite dark now. She will have to explore *her Tree* more tomorrow. For one thing, she wants to see what's in that hole the boy reached into. Surely she can take a little time to do that before setting out to find Summer. She reaches the top and, again, the leaves enfold her and the Tree sighs contentedly. Autumn puffs herself a pillow of cool air and settles down to wait for morning.

CHAPTER SIX

SUNDAY MORNING

"**S**mash her down! Smash her down!"

Billy wakes up soaked in sweat and yelling "Stop! Stop!" He's been dreaming about that old pickup truck, and in his dream it's twice as big and the grinding is four times as loud and it keeps crashing into the Tree, with those two grungy guys sitting inside and whooping and laughing and yelling "Smash her down! Smash her down!"

Punchy jumps onto the bed and nuzzles up against him. That feels good even though it makes Billy hotter. He calms down and sleeps the rest of the night, but his first thought in the morning is for his Tree. He'd like to go check on it, but there's not enough time before he and Pap leave for church.

For breakfast, Pap makes oatmeal and they have cold biscuits. Punchy eats a biscuit and some scraps of chicken from the refrigerator. He won't eat oatmeal.

As soon as they finish, Pap says, "You go on and get ready now, Billy Boy, we don't want to be late for church. We're already gonna miss Sunday School. I'll wash up these dishes. And try to get some of that dirt out of your hair."

Billy grins. They always miss Sunday School. But he does as he's told, washing up in the little bathroom, leaning over the tiny basin to brush his hair. He rinses his comb and pulls it through, but the hair sticks up anyway.

He looks at himself in the bathroom mirror. Going by the pencil marks Pap's made alongside the mirror, he's gotten taller. Maybe he'll be real tall like his daddy was. Or maybe he'll not get much taller, will be more Pap's size. Either way, he guesses he'll be skinny all his life, since every man relative he's ever seen or seen a picture of was a bean pole.

When Billy goes back into his bedroom, he stops at the picture of Mama and Daddy that sits on top of the chest of drawers. Daddy, strong and handsome, grinning at Mama. Mama looking pretty, smiling a big smile at the camera. Mr. and Mrs. Burnette, just married. Will and Allie. Billy touches his wristband and runs his finger over the initials. WAB. William Alvan Burnette. Daddy only lived for four years after that picture was taken. He drowned in the Gulf when Billy was just three. Grandpap said he got caught in the undertow. So Billy's not supposed to go swimming down there unless Grandpap is with him.

There's a picture of Mama in her high school cheerleading uniform. And one of Pap and Grandmam when they were young. She was holding baby Will, and had on a dress she told Billy she'd made out of a flour sack. It had little flowers on it. Grandmam was good at sewing. She was good at everything. It's two years since she died and he still misses her every day.

Billy opens a drawer and finds a clean brown-checked shirt and some brown pants that aren't too dirty. There aren't any clean socks. Well, Pap isn't one to notice that sort of thing. In fact, sometimes Pap can't find clean socks for himself. They need to get a load of clothes washed and hung out to dry. He'll remind Pap tomorrow, if he thinks of it. Billy's got too much else on his mind right now. He pulls his brown oxfords out from under the bed and sits on the floor to put them on. They're scuffed and too tight and the laces are frayed. His feet have grown and he knows Pap can't afford to buy him new shoes. They'll have to wait until Mama sends some more money.

"Time to go, Billy Boy. Come on now," Pap calls. He's already sitting in Big Beulah when Billy runs down the steps.

They make it to church just in time for the service. Afterwards, Billy fidgets when Miz Garraway collars Pap, like she always does. She gives Pap a basket of food, like she always does. And, like she always does, asks how are things going and what has he heard from Billy's mother. Pap says things are going fine, like he always does, and that Allie's still working at the cafe up in Crowley and still living in her family's old homestead and she calls regular and she'll be coming down in a week or two, and much obliged to you for asking, and for the vittles, and we need to be getting on back to see to things.

Some other folks want to say hello, but don't hold them up long.

The drive home takes a while longer because the old car overheats. It's not that much of a problem—it overheats pretty often and Pap always keeps a big stoppered jug of water in the trunk, just in case. He has to wait until the radiator cools off some before pouring it in, so Billy gets out of the car. They've just passed a dead armadillo on the side of the road and he walks back to get a closer look at it.

"Can I take him home and bury him, Pap?" he yells.

"Naw, son, we don't need no dead armadillos. We got enough live ones rootin' round the place."

Billy feels sorry for the critter. It looks so pitiful, lying there on its grey armored back with its reddish underside showing and its little legs stiff and sticking straight up. He pulls it over away from the road and into some bushes. He wishes he could give it a decent burial.

But what he most wishes is that Pap would get Big Beulah going and get them on home so he and Punchy can go see if those guys have been back to the Tree.

CHAPTER SEVEN

REBELLION

Autumn awakes with a start on Sunday morning. It takes her a few seconds to remember where she is. Ah, at the top of the big, old, hospitable Tree. *Her Tree.* She hadn't intended to go to sleep at all; she'd meant to watch the world light up with the morning rise of Sol. She's snuggled in this lovely cocoon of leaves, so comfortable she has to force herself to move branches out of the way and upstretch. When she does, she sees blue sky above and trees all around. The ones to the south are smaller, even scrawny, and there aren't as many of those.

It is very hot. She swizzles her head to puff cool air around her neck, then looks up to check on Sol. He's almost at the top of the sky. For the second time in a row, she has slept too much of the day away. The heat must be what's tiring her. It's time to get busy. She has to find that wayward Weatherling Summer and send her on her way. Wayward Weatherling. Autumn likes the way that sounds.

She looks south again. Past the trees, there's a road. Beyond that, there are huge mounds, very white, with patches of long yellow grass on and around them. The grass is waving; there must be a breeze down there. Well, that would be nice. She stretches higher to look past the mounds. Water. A lot of water. The most water she has ever seen all in one place.

Autumn starts down the Tree, enjoying the slide from branch to branch, staying near the big trunk and feeling its scaly, brown bark. She stops at the hole she'd seen the boy look into, but draws her hand away from it when Mama N's words come to her: *stay focused.* She keeps her fingers on the trunk, though, stretching her arm long enough to feel the back of the Tree between the branches as she goes down. She's almost to the bottom when her fingers touch something different. She can't resist moving around to see what it is.

A heart has been cut into the Tree. There are letters inside it. She looks closely. SJB loves AJB. She feels the letters with a fingertip and hears her Tree sigh. Is it a sad sigh or a happy sigh? She isn't sure. It's different from the welcoming sigh she heard before. *STAY FOCUSED.* Mama N's words are louder in her mind this time. Autumn sighs too, a not-so-happy sigh, and slides to the ground.

The water she saw from above draws her in that direction. She doesn't know why, other than it's as good a direction as any if you don't know where you're going to begin with. And she has to admit to herself that she's curious about that water. Plus, she'd like to dip her toes into something cool. She crosses the road. It's paved, but sand has blown onto it. Later, she'll have to see where it goes. For now, she wants to go straight to the water. The way the crow flies, as Mama N is fond of saying. The only crows Autumn ever saw were just circling around or sitting in trees or on one of those things Jack Frost calls scarecrows. And making an awful racket with their cawing. But of course, she never said any of that to Mama N.

There aren't any trees beyond the road. She upstretches slightly so she can see over the tall grass as she moves through the mounds. When she comes out of the grass she is almost blinded by the reflection of Sol off of sand. This is the most sand and the whitest sand she's ever seen. She kneels down and sifts some through her fingers. Fine grains, soft and clean. A little breeze blows them away as they fall from her hands. The sandy strip goes down to the water and makes a wide, beautiful path alongside it, as far as she can see to the left and to the right. The water is *everywhere* beyond it, stretching out south, east and west.

What in the name of All Abundance is this? Do rivers grow so big? Or do all the rivers in the world flow down to this place? She sits on the sand and closes her eyes, loving the feel of the water as it laps up around her feet. The soft laplets, the warm, salty air, the brilliant blue-green of the water and the bright, blue sky are so soothing that, for the moment, Autumn forgets why she's there. She is called back to her mission by the raucous squawk of a big white bird that has come up on her right side. His head is cocked at her, as if to ask what business she has being there.

"Hello," says Autumn. No response. "I'm a Weatherling." No response. "I'm looking for someone." He just looks at her. Perhaps her Nature Link with birds doesn't extend to Deep South birds.

She tries again. "Have you seen anyone who maybe looks sort of like me?" She wishes she could give a better description, but she's never actually seen a Summer Weatherling.

The bird says nothing. He turns his back on her and looks off down the sand, to the right. She looks, too, and sees a hazy form—no, two hazy forms—approaching. The glare from the sand is blinding. She gets up and walks that way, shading her eyes. The forms begin to take shape. One is short and is wearing a red cape. As they get close, a blast of very hot air hits Autumn. She tingles with excitement.

"Hey," she calls out, "is one of you, by any chance, Summer 1949?"

"I'm Summer," says the smaller one. The tall, light-blue one doesn't say anything, but bends back and forth, gently blowing a bit of very welcome cool air.

"I don't believe this!" Autumn bounces up and down on the sand, splashing the laplets around her feet. "I'm Autumn 1949! I've found you and I didn't even know where to look! It was the Tree! The Tree showed me. I landed on top of it last night and it's so tall that when Sol came up this morning, I could see forever and I spied this world of water, and *dazzling daylight,* I was drawn straight to here!"

Summer does not look happy. Her blue companion moves away and upstretches, bending back and forth gracefully, making no sound. Autumn finally winds down and Summer speaks.

"What are you doing here?"

"I'm here to take over," says Autumn. You're way overdue back at Nature Quarters. Mama N is really upset that you've stayed here so long. Summer Time is over. Well, it *should* be over. I need to get busy cooling things off and getting leaves off trees and..." She can't think what else she's supposed to do. She knows there's more, but her training was spotty and ended so abruptly.

"I'm not leaving," says Summer.

"But you have to. Mama N says so."

"I don't care what Mother-Who-Thinks-She's-Boss-of-Everything-Nature said. I no longer work for her. I like it here and I'm staying. Just skydoodle back to wherever she is now and tell her that."

Autumn is stunned. "But it's my turn," she says. "Mother Nature has the say as to what happens when, and this is when I am supposed to be here. And, anyway, I don't think you can just quit."

"Yes, she can." The cool, musical voice comes from Summer's tall companion. "She can and she will. She has. Just go back and tell that to your dictatorial old boss. The Deep South is a great place and we're going to make sure it stays great. No more cold weather here."

"I don't bring cold weather. Autumn Time is not cold. It's cool and pleasant, not cold at all." Autumn is getting irritated.

"Ah, but you pave the way for cold weather and we don't like cold weather. Nobody in the Deep South likes Winter Time and they don't want to have it anymore," says the cool voice.

"Just who are you, anyway?" asks Autumn.

"He's a Weatherling and he's my friend." Summer turns, outstretches her hand to him. "This is Gulf Breeze. We make a great team. We're going to rule here forever. So you can just get yourself off to some place you're wanted."

Autumn doesn't know what to say. The training manual didn't mention anything like this. It seems like some sort of revolt. What in the World of Nature is she supposed to do about it? She sits down on the wet sand, burrows her feet in it, and closes her eyes to think. When she opens them, the big white bird is back at her side, looking at her with head cocked, and Summer and Gulf Breeze have disappeared.

CHAPTER EIGHT

PUFFS OF AIR

"That woman sure can cook, Billy Boy." Pap is eating one of Miz Garraway's fried drumsticks. Billy's finishing a big helping of banana pudding. They're at the table in the kitchen, still wearing their church clothes, except Pap has taken off his tie and his suit coat. Punchy is getting the last bits of chicken out of his dish in the corner.

"You're right, Pap. She a real good cook. She makes the best banana pudding I ever ate. Besides Grandmam's, I mean." Billy doesn't want to get into an argument with his grandpap on the subject, but the truth is, Grandmam never put enough bananas in her pudding and Miz Garraway's is always just loaded with them.

All in all, he'd say Miz Garraway was as good a cook as Grandmam, except for her cornbread. Nobody could beat Grandmam's buttermilk cornbread, cooked in the big iron skillet and all crunchy on the outside. He misses that cornbread. He misses her. They don't visit the two graves in the churchyard cemetery—hers and Billy's daddy's—on Sundays, but once a month they go there during the week and Pap pulls weeds and if they have any flowers blooming, they take some. He knows Pap misses her something awful and is still grieving for his son, too.

Billy finishes his banana pudding in a hurry. He would like some more, but he and Punchy need to get down to the Tree. He looks over at the stack of breakfast dishes and then at the ones they've just used. Pap is gnawing on that drumstick and looking like his mind has drifted off a million miles away.

"Pap, is it okay if I wash these dishes later? I got to get out and run some. Seems like I been sitting all day."

"You just about have, boy. Do 'em later. I'm gonna have some banana pudding and then take me a little nap. You and Punchy go on."

The two are off like a shot, down the road to the myrtle bushes and into the oaks and running along Lost Lane to the Tree. They slow down as they get closer to it and silently push into the heavy bushes. Billy goes just far enough to see the Tree, but still stay hidden. There it is, safe and sound. No pickup truck. Nobody around. He and Punchy go and sit down under it. Billy gets comfortable, with his back up against the Tree. Everything is okay. It's just another quiet, ordinary Sunday afternoon.

It's awful hot, though, even under the big Tree.

"Golly, Punchy," Billy says, "Pap's right. Shoot, it's hot as *two* blast furnaces. I wish it'd cool off some." He unbuttons his shirt and flaps it to stir up some air.

Well, there's at least one person in the Deep South who doesn't want hot weather all the time. Autumn has landed in a tall pine tree not far from the big magnolia just in time to see Billy and Punchy come out from the bushes. She's heard Billy say he wishes it would cool off. Talking about blast furnaces again. She'd sure like to see a blast furnace and feel how hot it was. Autumn shakes her head. What she needs to be thinking about is whether the boy and the dog might be able to help her re-find Summer.

She has to try and make friends with them. The boy wasn't able to see her before, when they were both in the Tree. The dog might have, though. He sure acted like he knew she was there. Maybe just from her scent. She knows dogs have a keen sense of smell. Up North, dogs could see her, but this is a Deep South dog. Maybe he's different. And if he *could* see her, would he understand her Nature Language? She has never tried talking to a dog.

Autumn slides down the pine and stands under a small, spreading mimosa tree. Punchy jumps up, looking straight at her. She isn't sure whether it's a friendly look or a fierce look. She stayed a safe distance from Up North dogs because she heard they sometimes could be difficult. Of course, her training hadn't covered dogs.

Punchy nudges Billy with his nose and whines, then looks straight back at Autumn and barks. He sees her, all right. He's trying to tell the boy she's there.

"Hey, quit that!" Billy's ready for a rest after all that Sunday dinner he ate and the run through Lost Lane, and here's Punchy pushing at his hand, licking his face, whining and wriggling, then running off a few feet, toward a mimosa tree.

"Is there something over there, fella? Well, whatcha waitin' for? Go on and see. Go on, I'm coming." But Punchy waits until Billy gets up and then presses against his leg as they walk to the little tree. Autumn draws back and floats up into it. Punchy's eyes follow her. He props his paws on the trunk and whines.

"I don't see anything," said Billy.

Autumn knows he's able to feel something, though. She stretches her neck down and sends a puff of cool air onto his head.

"Hey!" Billy reaches up to his hair, then holds his hand up in the air. "I just felt cool air, Punch. Didn't last long, though."

He feels another puff, this time on his cheek. "There it is again!"

Punchy is still looking up and whining. Billy gives the thin tree trunk a good shake.

"Nothing coming down. And I don't see a thing." He touches his cheek and remembers the cool stream of air he'd felt in the Tree the day before. He looks all around, shakes his head. "Well, anyway, the Tree's all right. I got to get those dishes washed and do my homework for tomorrow." And, he needs to find something for Pap to do so he won't get to thinking about whatever's worrying him and start in drinking.

"Come on, Punch."

Billy is through the thick bushes before he realizes Punchy isn't with him. He goes back. The little dog is still at the mimosa, pawing at its trunk.

"I know you think you've treed something, Punchy. I don't know what it is, but we gotta go. Maybe it'll still be here tomorrow." Billy looks up once more. A cool puff comes down and then something wispy, like a spider web, brushes his face. He jumps back and feels his cheeks. Nothing is there. He shivers. Autumn knows she has startled him with her cape and draws back. She doesn't want to scare him, just wants to find a way to communicate with him.

But that brush across his face has made up Billy's mind. "Come on, Punchy, let's get out of here."

Punchy looks at Billy, then back up into the mimosa. Autumn, peering down at him, decides he definitely is not fierce. He's curious, like her. She downstretches her hand and touches his head.

"I'll see you tomorrow," she says. "Now, go on."

Punchy gives a sharp bark. He bounds away to Billy and the two of them head for home.

CHAPTER NINE

FAT MAN AND PIMPLES

Autumn watches Billy and Punchy go through the bushes and disappear into the oaks. She looks up. Sol is well over to the west. Sunday is going by too fast. *I need to look for Summer*, she thinks, and whooshes up to the top of her big Tree. She upstretches herself tall and looks in every direction, but decides it's too late in the day, so draws back and settles down in her treetop bed. She'll get all rested up and start out at first daylight.

She doesn't sleep long. BZZZZZZZ. The noise is enough to wake a hibernating bear. Her Tree is vibrating. And shuddering. What in the name of All Abundance is going on? It's not completely dark, because there are so many stars out, but she can't see anything at the base of the tree because of the thick leaves. She listens for a moment, then slides her way down.

There's a truck pulled up close to the Tree's trunk, with its headlights shining on it. And two men. One is holding a long buzzing thing against her Tree. Oh, *striking stars*, are they hurting it? She gets closer and can see that the buzzing thing is cutting into bark.

She remembers a group of men who were cutting down trees in a forest Up North. Mama N said that's what they did for a living and that the pieces would be used for houses and if they had any sense they'd grow more trees. But that was happening in the daytime and this was at night. These men couldn't be trying to cut down her Tree—it was way too big—but why would they want to hurt it?

The buzzing stops. She doesn't like the looks of the men. She doesn't like the way they sound, either.

"Dadburnit!" the skinny one says in a thin, whiny voice.

"Whatcha stopping for, Sport?" asks the fat one, his voice low and growly. "We ain't got all night, you know. It's going on eleven o'clock already."

"I didn't stop, Mac. The saw just quit on me. Must be something wrong with it. Did you ever use it after you borrowed it from that guy last month?"

"Yeah, I used it and it's been in that toolbox on the truck ever since, right where I told you it was last night. Lemme see that thing. You ain't ruined it, have you? You ever use a chain saw before?" Mac reaches over and fiddles with the start button on the saw, then shakes it. "You idiot, it's outta gas. Get the can from the truck."

"You get it. I'm tired. That saw's heavy. Anyhow, it's your truck and your gas."

"No, it's your gas, Sport. You bought it. Now get it and fill up the saw. You should've done that to start with."

"I didn't buy the gas, you bought the gas, Mac. Remember? You said you was going to go by the filling station last night."

"No, you idiot, you was supposed to get it when you borrowed the truck to take your ma to church this morning. Now we're gonna have to siphon some from the truck."

Sport clears his throat and spits. "There may not be all that much gas in your truck, Mac."

"What do you mean?" Mac narrows his eyes. "How much driving around did you do today?"

"Well, when we got back from church, Ma wanted to go pick up some stuff from a friend of hers over at Chapka. I didn't think anything about the gas since you said you was going by the station to get some for the saw. I figured everything was full up. It ain't my fault you didn't do it. If you'd get the gas gauge fixed, you'd know

₃ about empty. Anyhow, we wasn't supposed to start the job
₁₁ tomorrow night. That's what the old man said."

Mac sits down under the tree and puts his head in his hands.
"How'd I get such a dummy for a nephew? When you gonna get
your old car fixed? Use it to take your ma places? And when you
gonna get a job—how about that? Quit sponging off her and hanging
around the pool hall all the time. When you gonna do that, huh?
Cheez, you're 23 years old.

"Yeah, Sport, the old man did say start tomorrow, but he wants
us finished up by Wednesday and yesterday when I saw how big
the durn thing is, I figured we'd better get on it quick as we could.
It's going to take a good long while to saw six inches into it all the
way around. That thing is humongous. Well, thanks to you, we've
wasted all this time. Come on, let's see if we got enough gas to get
us to the truck stop up the highway. The fillin' station in Lettston
ain't going to be open on Sunday night."

"We comin' back here after you get it, Mac?"

"Naw, it's too late and I'm too tired and my knee is acting up
again." Mac hangs his head and shakes it slowly. "We'll have to
get back down tomorrow night." He pushes himself up from the
ground, favoring his left knee, and they climb into the truck. The
motor grinds when he turns the key, then starts.

Autumn shivers as they drive away. They mean to keep hurting
her Tree. She climbs down to the ground and outstretches her arms
until her hands meet around the huge trunk. She feels it shake as
she hugs it.

"Don't worry, I'll do something," she says. "I'll do something."

CHAPTER TEN

PUNCHY MEETS AUTUMN

"**H**ey, slow down, Punchy!"

Every morning when Billy goes down the road to catch the bus for school, Punchy goes right along with him. They usually get sidetracked on the way and make it just in time. Monday morning, though, Punchy doesn't show much interest in the dead crow or the huge new ant hill. Billy doesn't either. He pushes the crow under some bushes and keeps moving.

The two little girls are already waiting for the bus in front of the Showers' house. They're twins, six years old. May and Fay. They look just alike and dress just alike and Billy can't tell them apart. Their house is a little farther along the road. They act shy with Billy, but they love Punchy. They make a big fuss over him when he runs up. Two bigger boys, Al and Sam Phelps, come through the cow pasture alongside the house.

Rick hasn't come out yet. He has chores to do before school. He's twelve, like Billy, but smaller. His hair is coal black. His left leg is twisted from having polio when he was nine and he limps. Some of the kids tease him about it, but he can walk okay and can run as fast as most of them. He's real smart, too. When the Showers bought the old dairy farm and moved there three months ago he and Billy became friends right away.

Rick appears just as the bus pulls up. It's already nearly full of kids. Mr. Davis opens the door and the little girls get on first. Rick and Billy pat Punchy on the head and tell him goodbye. The four boys get on and Mr. Davis closes the door. They head down the gravel road and, after a mile, turn left toward the school onto the paved county road.

Punchy waits until the bus pulls away, then heads for Lost Lane. He doesn't know what that was in the mimosa tree the day before, but he's going to see if it's still there.

After the fat guy and the skinny guy drive away in the very early hours of Monday morning, Autumn goes back to her perch at the top of the Tree. She wants to do some thinking. First, about those two guys, then about Summer, then about Mama N.

She needs to take care of the Tree but she also has to find Summer and get her to skydoodle out of the Deep South and she doesn't know how to do either one and Mama N is depending on her and will be disappointed in her and maybe fire her and.... Too many ands. They whirl around in her mind until she's dizzy. Finally, worn out with it all, she goes back to sleep.

When she wakes up, she's calm. Her mind is clear. She's confident she'll be able to think up a plan. Two plans. One to save her Tree and one to get rid of Summer. As she lies there, she hears little whiny noises coming from down below and she hopes she knows who's making them. She glides down to the bottom branches of the Tree and there's that little dog, scratching at the bark, looking up at her, wagging his short tail.

"Hi there, Punchy," she says, and floats down to the ground.

Punchy yips once, then sits and looks like he's waiting for her to say more.

"Can you talk to me?" Autumn asks.

He yips again.

"Guess not. Maybe I'll have to learn barking." She doesn't know, but she thinks it might be a possibility. There must be a dog-talk Nature course.

"Well, Punchy, I know your name, but you don't know mine. I'm Autumn. I'm a Weatherling."

Punchy barks and jumps up to put his paws on her, but she's suddenly not there. He must have scared her. She moves so fast, she's in the tree again. He sits back on his haunches, looks up at her, whines. He has seen someone like this at the beach, only shorter and rounder. And, though he's not good with colors, this one's cape doesn't look the same.

Punchy and Billy like the beach. Rick does, too. Pap tells people it's too much sun and too much sand for his old skin and bones, but of course everybody knows it's because of what happened to his son. Billy does go in the water sometimes without Pap knowing it, but he's careful not to go very far out. Rick isn't supposed to ever go to the beach without an adult because of his leg, and his parents are usually too busy to take him. Punchy goes a lot when Billy's at school or church.

Autumn comes down out of the tree and blows a little cool air at Punchy. The shorter one had blown hot air. Very hot air. And had said, "Go away, dog."

"Punchy, somebody has been hurting my Tree. Cutting it with a long buzzing thing. The thing stopped working so they left, but they're coming back." She waits to see if he gives any sign of understanding.

The little dog barks once and tries to take hold of her cape, but it flutters out of his reach. He turns and heads for Lost Lane. Autumn sighs—he's leaving. But no, he stops, looks at her, barks again. He wants her to come with him. She follows him to the hidden path in the woods. She's pretty sure now they have a Nature link. He can't say words, but he seems to understand her—maybe just her feelings, but there's a link.

She looks around the lane. What a beautiful place. Quiet and peaceful. The trees keep some of Sol's heat out. Autumn thinks it may be the coolest place in the Deep South.

When they get to the little house, Punchy runs up the dirt driveway and Autumn sees Pap sitting in one of the two white slatted chairs on the porch. He's rocking back and forth. She hasn't seen this kind of chair anywhere else. It looks like fun. The night before there wasn't time to notice everything. There's a swing on the far end, and a little flower box on each side of the door. The flowers don't look healthy. Autumn hangs back as Punchy bounds up the steps to Pap.

Pap sure is a skinny little old man. Just about bald-headed, but some gray hair hangs down to his neck in the back. He's wearing faded gray overalls with big shoulder straps and a washed-out blue plaid shirt. His boots are cracked and caked with dried mud.

Pap pats his lap and Punchy jumps up on it, panting. He rubs Punchy's head and neck. "Good fellow, good fellow. Where you been? You need some water." He lifts the little dog down and gets up to fill the water bowl from the bucket. Punchy laps at it like he's dying of thirst. When he gets enough, he goes to where Autumn is standing on the top step and barks.

"What?" Pap walks over to him, then looks up at the sky. "Whoo, what time is it? Well pretty nigh noon, it looks like. I just been sittin' around. It's too hot to do anything." He looks at the thermometer hanging by the door. "Still in the high nineties. October third. Seems like summer ain't never gonna end. Well, I better rustle us up a little something to eat. Come on, boy."

Punchy doesn't move; he's looking at Autumn.

"All right, stay out here if you want to. I think I'll make me a baloney sandwich. I guess you'll let me know when you get hungry."

As soon as he goes inside, Autumn comes up on the porch. She wants to try out that rocking chair.

CHAPTER ELEVEN

SCHOOL BUS

"You have a good time at your Aunt Dora's, Rick?" Billy and his friend are sitting in their fifth row seat, where they're usually safe from the Randall brothers, who always claim the bench that goes across the back of the bus.

"Oh man, it was great! I love it up there in Strockville. I wish we coulda stayed longer. I got to see all my cousins and aunts and uncles on Daddy's side. Uncle James took us to the swimming hole both days. Man, that water was cold! And I never seen so much food in my life. Everybody brought food. We was eatin' all the time and man, it was good! I wish you coulda been there."

"I wish I had some cousins," Billy says. "And some aunts and uncles, too. Well, I do have one uncle: Mama's brother. Uncle Shay. He lives in Florida. He came to see us about three years ago. Brought me a knife with a handle shaped like a gator. Mama took it away, said I wasn't old enough, but shoot, I was nine. I don't know what she did with it. I could sure use a good knife. I don't know if Uncle Shay will ever come back. Pap says he will, but I don't know. We don't hear anything from him. Well, Mama probably does."

"Wow! A gator handle! You ought to ask her about it again. Hey, Florida's not that far, is it? You can see on the map it's right under Alabama. Well, under part of Alabama. The Gulf's under this part. Why don't you get your grandpap to take you down there and you can get yourself another gator knife."

"Naw, I asked Pap about going and he said Big Beulah would never make it. Uncle Shay's all the way down at the end of Florida. Very tip end. Lives on an island. There's a bunch of little islands. They've hooked 'em up so you can drive all the way down now. They call 'em keys."

"Funny thing to call islands," says Rick.

Suddenly, hands close on Billy's and Rick's necks.

"Well, well, who do we have here? Silly Boy and his sidekick, Rickety, talking about islands! Whadda you two twerps know about islands?" The Randalls have moved in right behind them. The twins were in that seat before; the Randalls must have made them go to the back.

"Lemme go." Billy grabs at the big hands squeezing his neck.

"Oooh, am I hurting itsy, bitsy Silly Boy?" Matt Randall squeezes tighter and laughs.

Rick is making little choking sounds, with his hands clenched at his sides and his face turning red. "Look a here, Matt," says Roy Randall. "This one sounds like a old croaker. I guess I done caught me a old croaker fish and I didn't even need a hook."

Matt tightens his grip on Billy. "When you gonna give me that old scrawny dog? I need me a good hunter. You ain't got no use for him."

"We hunt him all the time." Billy coughs the words out. He keeps pulling at Matt's wrists.

The bus stops to let some more kids on. Mr. Davis shifts to neutral, pulls the emergency brake and turns around to look at them.

"You Randalls let loose of those boys and get yourselves up here to the front."

"We ain't hurtin' nobody," says Roy.

"We just horsing around, Mr. Davis. Havin' us some fun with our buddies here," says Matt. But he turns loose and so does Roy.

They flop back in the seat and look at the bus driver like they're daring him to try to make them move.

Mr. Davis stands up. He's a big man. "I ain't toleratin' no foolishness on this bus. You get on up here." He motions for the two small boys in the seat right behind him to move to the back.

The Randalls look like they're thinking about it. Then Matt grins and slaps Roy on the shoulder. "Oh come on, let's make the man happy." They swagger up to the front, elbowing the kids in aisle seats and bumping into the boys who are changing seats. Laughing like they've put a big one over on somebody. When they sit down behind Mr. Davis, he releases the emergency brake, puts the bus in gear and they start on down the road.

Rick is rubbing his neck. "He 'bout choked me to death. I thought I was a goner this time."

"You're okay," says Billy. "Maybe they'll find somebody else to torment on the way back." Billy has other things on his mind. "Rick, can you come home with me after school? There's something I want to tell you about. I may need your help."

"Mama's already said it's okay. She figured we'd want to talk about Strockville. Can't stay real long, though, I gotta tend to the goats before it gets dark. What've you got to tell me?"

"Can't tell you now. But it's important. I think it might be something bad."

It's one of the longest school days either one of them has ever had. Billy is worried, rubbing his wristband a lot, anxious to get back to the Tree. Rick is excited at the idea of his friend needing help with something and that the something might be something bad. It seems like a day and a half before they're back on the bus. The Randalls don't bother them this time, except for Roy cuffing Rick on the head on his way to the back bench.

When they get out at the bus stop, Rick, in his limping run, hurries in to tell his mother he's for sure going to Billy's and comes out with six peanut butter cookies still warm from the oven.

"Hey, where's Punchy, Billy?"

"Maybe Pap has him off hunting squirrels." Billy frowns. It always worries him a little when Punchy isn't waiting for him at the bus stop.

The boys run alongside the gravel road. Rick, even with his limp, never has any trouble keeping up. They don't say anything until they finish Miz Showers' cookies. Rick eats faster because he's so anxious to hear Billy's news.

"So tell me," he says, when he's gulped down his last bite. "What's going on?"

"Wait 'til after we check in with Pap," Billy says through a mouthful of cookie. "Then we'll go down to the Tree. The Tree's what I'm worried about."

Rick knows the magnolia tree, of course. He's been there lots. But he doesn't know about Lost Lane. Billy has started to tell him a couple of times, but for some reason he can't bring himself to share his and Punchy's and Grandmam's secret place. Grandmam showed it to Billy not long before she died. She said to keep it for himself and Punchy. That everybody should have a special place to be all alone when they needed it.

Lost Lane and the Tree. Grandmam's two special places. She had turned both of them over to him. A lot of people knew about the Tree, it being so old and the biggest magnolia tree in the state. But they hadn't spent hours up in it, like Billy.

When the boys get to the house, Billy's surprised to see Punchy sitting on the porch by Grandmam's rocker. He kneels down on the ground. "Hey boy, where you been? How come you weren't at the bus stop? You and Pap been hunting? Come here, boy." Punchy runs down the steps, jumps on him, licks his face, and looks back at the rocker. It's rocking. Slowly.

Rick kneels down too, to pet the little dog. "Hey there, Punchy. How you doing? You miss me? You gonna give me a lick, too?"

Punchy obliges, then runs back up on the porch to the rocking chair. The boys follow him.

"I'll tell Pap we're here," says Billy, and goes inside.

His friend looks over at Punchy and the chair. It stops rocking. "You been up in that chair, Punchy?" Rick walks over and sits down in it.

Punchy backs up. Autumn's in that chair. She had been rocking hard, but when the boys came up on the porch she slowed down. Now it looks like maybe Rick has squashed her. Punchy whines and dances around, trying to see what's left of her under Rick's backside.

"I'm over here," Autumn's sitting on the porch rail, by the water bucket. Punchy had forgotten how fast she can move. He runs to her and starts barking.

Pap sticks his head out the screen door. "Come on in, Rick. You fellows need something cold to drink. We got milk. Maybe we can rustle up some cookies." Rick is red-faced from running, and sweaty, and still hungry and that sounds good to him. To Billy, too.

"Glad you're back, boy," says Pap. "You catch any fish up there in Strockville?"

Punchy doesn't follow them into the house. He's back by the rocker again, doing a little dance and looking up at it. It's rocking again.

Autumn is thinking as she rocks. She still needs a plan. "Punchy, we've got to get your boy to the Tree so he can see what those guys did to it," she says.

That turns out to be easy. In a few minutes, the two friends come through the screen door, Billy calling back over his shoulder, "We're goin' down to the Tree for a while, Pap."

While Pap was talking with Rick about Strockville, Billy had made up his mind about something. He wants to get to the Tree as fast as he can; he doesn't want to take the long way around. He's going to have to tell Rick about Lost Lane.

They're down the steps and starting to run before Billy realizes that Punchy isn't with them. He turns. Punchy's at the top of the steps, looking back and forth between the boys and Grandmam's rocker. The rocker is rocking really fast. There is no wind. Billy watches and wonders. For some reason, those cool puffs of air come into his mind. He whistles to his dog.

"Let's go, Punchy."

The rocking stops. "Go with them," says Autumn. "I'll be there in just a bit." She wants to find out more about Pap. She knows the boys will see the gash on the Tree.

Punchy takes off. At the end of the driveway, Rick turns to the right, heading up the road. "No." Billy says. "We're going a shorter way." Rick starts to ask a question, but Billy shushes him and the three turn left and run fast until they get to the wax myrtle bushes. Billy stops there.

"I'm going to show you something, Rick. But you gotta promise you won't tell anybody else. Not anybody. You promise?"

Rick's face lights up. His finger swipes twice across his chest. "Cross my heart," he says.

CHAPTER TWELVE

PAP

"**N**ot a care in the world," Pap says it out loud as he watches the boys run down the road with Punchy at their heels. "Well, I got enough troubles for all of us."

When they're out of sight, he goes back in the house and looks around.

He had spent some time that morning trying to clean up, but the place is still messy. Papers and bills are piled up on the radio table. He needs to go through all that. He needs to wash some clothes in the old wringer washing tub and get them hung out on the line. He should make a trip to the grocery store, too.

"Sally would sure be upset if she could see this," he says. Sally had kept everything neat as a pin. Miz Garraway was like that. Her house was near as clean as Sally's was, when Sally was alive. Them two had got along good. He hadn't liked Slim Garraway all that much, but Slim was gone these ten years or so, and Pap doesn't like to think ill of the dead.

He stands there in the front room and looks over at the corner cupboard. "I could use a shot of whiskey." He glances at the old clock on the mantle. "Lord, Alvan Burnett, it ain't even four o'clock yet. You can wait 'til after supper, surely." He knows he's been drinking too much. And when he thinks about how he yelled at Billy Boy and kicked at Punchy Saturday morning, he feels downright ashamed. What would Sally say about that, he wonders. Wonders? No, he knows what she'd say: *You ought to be ashamed,*

Alvan Burnette. What's come over you? You gotta straighten up and take care of that boy. That's what she'd say, all right. She's not here to say it, but he answers her, anyway.

"Well, Sally, if I could just get these money worries off me." He goes out to the little back porch and sits down on the old bench by the door, looking at the dried-out garden and mumbling to himself. With all the watering they're doing, that garden should be doing better, even in this blasted heat. Well, he can't do much more than he's already doing around the place. His heart and lungs have gotten bad and his back is always iffy.

Billy Boy's a good worker, but he has his schoolwork and he has to have some time to play, to just be a boy. "Poor kid don't even have a bicycle anymore. Every boy ought to have a bicycle, dadgum it," Pap says.

But the truth is, there's hardly any money coming in. Just his pension from the railroad; that don't go far these days. And what little bit Billy's mama can send for clothes for the boy. All the good farmland's been sold long ago.

"I need that fifteen thousand dollars bad, Sally," he says, "and I ain't going to get it until something's done about that old magnolia tree. Biggest magnolia in the state, so they've passed a law that it can't be cut down. The people who want to buy the strip of land don't want the tree on it and they know the government ain't gonna let 'em get rid of it."

But last month the real estate man had said, "If something should happen to that old tree, call me. You get my meaning?" And he'd given Pap a wink. That had put the idea in Pap's head. Just like the man meant it to.

"Now if them two guys'll just do what I've hired 'em to do. It already looks like they don't take orders so good," he says.

CHAPTER THIRTEEN

THE GASH ON THE TREE

"It looks alright to me," says Billy.

He and Rick have come out of the bushes breathing hard from their run and have stopped to catch their breath. Punchy doesn't stop. He runs to the Tree and all the way around it, sniffing the ground, looking up into the branches.

"Punch, are you still seeing things?" Billy's glad the little dog isn't showing any interest in the mimosa today. He and Rick move closer to the big Tree. It seems fine as they approach it, but when they get to the walkup limb they see the damage just to the left of it and a bit higher up.

"It *is* hurt!" Billy feels the gash. It's about a foot long but not very deep. There's sawdust around it and some on the ground, too.

Rick runs his fingers over it. "Looks to me like somebody's been using a chain saw on it. Oh man, who'd want to cut down your Tree? Couldn't do it, anyways—it's too big."

"They're probably trying to girdle it. That's when you cut in deep all the way around and the tree dies. Maybe they got started and saw it was impossible and gave up," says Billy. In his mind he sees Pap and those two guys. "I need to tell you what's been going on, Rick."

The boys sit down on the ground. Billy describes Pap's meeting with Fat Man and Pimples, and tells about seeing the pickup at the Tree afterwards. "It must be the Tree that's the job Pap's gonna pay them for, but I don't know why he's doing it. Why would he want to kill the Tree?"

Rick shakes his head. "I don't know. Oh man, that's terrible."

The boys get quiet. Punchy jumps onto Billy's lap and licks his nose.

"That dog's so dadgum smart," says Rick. "I think he understands every word you say."

Billy smiles. "He understands a lot, don't you, Punchy?"

Rick stands up and backs away, looking at the Tree. "Man, that's one big tree."

"Biggest magnolia in the state, they say."

"Boy howdy! That's special, ain't it!"

"Special for more than that, Rick. It blooms longer. Those prickle pods are bigger and have more seeds in them and stay hard longer. And that limb. You don't see a limb like that on a magnolia, big enough and flat enough to walk on. Leastways, I never saw or heard of one. It's a magnolia but in some ways it don't act just like a magnolia. My grandmam called it a magic magnolia." He looks sideways at Rick, waiting to see if he'll think that's nutty.

But Rick's looking at the tree and nodding. "Could be. Could be. It's sure different." He sits back down. "You think those guys'll come back?"

"I don't know, Rick, but I got to be down here tonight to see."

"What'll you do if they show up—sic Punchy on 'em?"

"Punchy ain't big enough to scare them off. Maybe noise would. Some kind of noise. Ghost sounds, maybe? Animal noises? Hitting rocks together? What do you think? Could you get down here to help me, Rick?"

"Oh man, yeah, I think so. But I don't see how just two of us can make enough noise. Ghost noises would be good, but how can we make them loud enough and scary enough? Too bad it ain't supposed to rain. A good storm could send 'em running for cover. I guess it'd have to keep up all night, though."

"We haven't had a storm in forever," says Billy. "Not likely to get one tonight."

The boys sit and think. Billy rubs his wristband. Traces the initials on it. WAB. William Alvan Burnette. His daddy. Punchy lies there with his head on his paws, watching Billy. Suddenly he sits up, looks over at the scrub oaks, and whines. Autumn is there! He runs over so fast that when she dodges he bumps his head on a tree.

"Good grief, Punch, watch where you're going," says Billy. "Maybe he ain't so smart after all."

While the boys laugh at him, Punchy sits back on his haunches and looks at Autumn.

"It's okay, Punchy," she says. "I've been up at the top of the oaks, listening. I think I know somebody who might be able to help. But I don't know where to find him. He's probably with Summer. If I can find her, maybe I'll find him, too."

Punchy's ears perk up. Autumn is kind of tall and wears a cape. He remembers seeing *somebody* at the beach that looked sort of like Autumn, but shorter. Wore a cape, too. That *somebody* was with another *somebody* who was tall and thin and bendy. Could they be the ones Autumn is talking about? If so, he can show her where he has seen them.

"Punchy, what are you doing over there? Come on back and help us think." Billy wants his little dog snuggled up in his lap. But Punchy stays where he is, gives a sharp bark, raises up on his hind legs, turns his head to one side and paws at the air.

"He's acting funny." Rick gets up, goes over to the dog, and tries to pick him up. Punchy twists away from him and takes off through the scrub oaks, toward the beach.

"Let him go, Rick. Maybe he's upset because I'm upset. Let him go. He probably needs a good run."

Punchy disappears from sight, with Autumn right beside him, heading for the place where he thinks they might find the two *somebodies*.

CHAPTER FOURTEEN

THE UNDERPIER

Autumn and Punchy run through the scrub oaks, then through the grass and great white mounds, on down to the flat, white sand. Punchy turns east as they get near the water and Autumn follows him.

Sol is well over to the west and Autumn is getting bored with running. It would be easier if she could just whoosh herself, but she can't figure out how to whoosh Punchy along with her without people seeing a dog that looks like he's flying through the air. Anyway, he can't tell her where they're going. He has to show her. The hot sand doesn't seem to bother his paws, but she floats up every now and then and blows cool air on her feet. It would be nice to soak them in the Gulf water, but Punchy stays on dry sand, and she stays with him. A man and woman are standing at the edge of the water, fishing. Two little kids playing in the sand call out, trying to get Punchy to come to them, but he runs by as fast as his short legs will carry him.

Up ahead, Autumn can see a long, wooden walkway, held up by tall, fat logs. It juts way out over the water. People are fishing on it. Punchy veers to the left and heads for where it starts on the sand, quite a distance from the water. Underneath that part, it's like a big, shady, no-wall room with small cracks between the planks overhead and lots of tucked-away places among the supporting logs. Punchy runs right under. Autumn decides to stay out in the sun and wait; she's afraid if Summer is really there and sees her, she'll take off again.

Punchy finds Summer right away. She's behind one of the big logs, sound asleep. He goes back out and, with a sharp bark, gets Autumn to follow him. Autumn kneels down by Summer. She says, very gently, "We need your help, Summer. Please wake up. We really need your help."

Summer is awake instantly, on her feet and turning to whoosh, when it registers on her what Autumn has said. She looks back.

"Is this some kind of trick?"

"It's nothing to do with getting you to leave." She paused to think how to convince Summer. "There's a big tree that some people want to cut down and we Weatherlings have to stop them. You and me and Gulf Breeze. Where is he?"

Summer shakes her head. "I'm not sure where he is. We had an argument and he left all huffy and puffy when Sol was just halfway across. I was tired from running from you and I've just been hanging around down here. GB would know what to do all right. He knows everything. *If* we decide to help." She looks at Punchy, then back at Autumn. "I've seen this dog before. Did he bring you here?"

"Oh, my earthly etiquette!" says Autumn. "Let me introduce you. This is Punchy. He did bring me to you. I told him you and Gulf Breeze might be able to save my...our...Tree. And you've been here in the Deep South so *long*, I guess he's seen you and knows where you hang out. Punchy, shake hands with Summer."

Punchy lifts a paw—Billy has taught him that trick—but apparently Summer doesn't know how to shake hands. Or doesn't want to. Anyway, he's glad he found her and he hopes that Gulf Breeze will come back on his own. He doesn't want to do any more looking right now. He lays down on the sand, rests his head on his paws, and pants.

"That dog needs some water," says Summer.

"There's a whole huge water hole right out there," Autumn says.

"Sheesh-cabubbles, you don't know anything, do you? That's saltwater, Dumdiddles. The Gulf is saltwater. He can't drink saltwater—nobody can. You gotta give him freshwater."

Punchy, still panting hard, lifts his head.

"Well, where do I find that, Miss Smarty?" asks Autumn. She's tired of Summer's attitude and, besides, she's getting hotter and hotter from being around her—such heat waves she gives off. Then Autumn thinks how much her Tree needs help and she puffs some cool air on herself and softens her tone.

"Oh look," she says, "I'm sorry. I hope you'll make some allowances for me. I'm new on the job and my training program was cut short and this whole place is so strange and I've got all these worries."

"Yeah, yeah, and I bet I know what your main problem is. Me. But you can forget about that one for now—this dog's gotta have water. There's not any here in the Underpier. Come on, Pokey, we'll find you some. You too, Miss Worrisome Weatherling. Make yourself useful for a change."

"Punchy," says Autumn. "His name is Punchy, not Pokey."

"Okay, whatever. But he's poked his nose into my business, bringing you to me, so maybe I'll just call him Pokey." Summer motions them to follow her. They leave the shelter of the Underpier and head north over the sand, which rises up gradually toward a large brown building. When they get closer, Autumn can see that it's made of wood and has a big porch and a big, wide-open door. There are people inside, sitting at tables, drinking from cups and bottles. Some are eating. Most are in bathing suits or shorts. It looks so shady and cool—it positively calls to her to come in. But Summer leads them to the side of the porch where there's a faucet sticking up, and no tables or chairs.

"Here we go. Get over here, Pokey. Oh wait a minute, let me find something to catch the water in. Oughta be something in here."

She goes to a tall wooden box, with no top, and downstretches her arms into it.

She sniffs. "Doesn't smell too bad." She pulls out some silvery paper and three dirty paper plates. She stacks the plates together, puts the paper on the bottom of them, brings it up over the sides and molds it into a bowl. "This'll work. This is aluminum foil—bet you didn't know that, did you, Fogbrain?"

She hands the makeshift doggie bowl to Autumn. "Hold this under the faucet while I turn the water on."

Autumn does know about aluminum foil, but she keeps her mouth shut. Summer is a Know-it-All, but in this case that's good—if she keeps thinking Autumn needs her, maybe she won't up and disappear again. So Autumn does as she is told. Summer turns the water to just a trickle so it won't splash out. When the bowl is full, Autumn puts it on the floor of the big porch, still holding the sides, making sure they don't collapse.

Punchy laps gratefully, occasionally turning his big brown eyes up to Autumn and then over to Summer. After he has his fill, he lies down and pants some more. Summer reaches back into the garbage box and pulls out something else. "It's half a hamburger and it looks fairly fresh. You want it, Pokey?" Punchy downs it in one gulp.

"Well, maybe I'll help you," says Summer. She upstretches herself very high to look around. "I don't see Gulf Breeze but I may know where to look. You two stay here."

"No," says Autumn. "You might disappear again and I don't know what I'll do if you don't help me. I'm going with you. Punchy, you go home. We'll come there after we locate Gulf Breeze. Let's skydoodle, Summer. We need to find him, pronto! We've got to save our Tree."

"Okay, okay, Miss Speedy Breakneck. See you later, Pokey!" And Summer takes off, sending a stream of very hot air onto Autumn's head.

As they leave, Punchy hears Summer ask, "What kind of word is pronto?" and Autumn replies, "Ask Gulf Breeze—he knows everything."

Punchy watches them whoosh up and away. Then he takes off for home.

CHAPTER FIFTEEN

BATTLE PLAN

Rick is sitting up against the tree, looking at Billy. "Okay, what are we going to do?"

"I don't know," says Billy. He's been pacing back and forth, but now he sits, too. "We got to get down here tonight and if they come back, stop them some way. But they're men and one of them's a big fellow. We need us a plan. First off, we got to get here before they do, but we can't come back 'til after dark. We just have to hope they don't show up until real late."

Rick thinks about that for a minute. "My folks go to sleep by nine o'clock 'cause they have to get up so early to milk. Their clock goes off at four thirty every morning. Mine goes off at six. Man, I hate that old alarm."

"How loud is it?" asks Billy.

"Too loud. Why?"

"I'm just thinking about how we could make us some noise. A loud alarm—that'd be good."

Rick smiles and nods. "Yeah! Two would be better, but I can't take theirs. You got one?"

"Pap does. I don't know for sure where it is. He don't use it; says he's got one in his head that wakes him up."

"Well, find it and wind it up good and bring it," says Rick.

"Yeah. But they won't sound as loud outside, will they? We need more stuff."

"How about if we put both clocks together and on some metal? That ought to make it louder. My mama has a big tin box for recipes. We could set them on it. Or in it. They'll ring a good long time if the alarms are wound up all the way. And how's about whistles? We both got whistles. Hey, know what? I can bring cowbells." Rick's getting more and more excited.

"How do we get it all going at once, Rick?"

"We'll have to figure that out. Where we going to be when we do this?"

"Yeah, good question." says Billy. "Maybe up in the Tree. Or one of these other trees. In the bushes. I don't know."

"What if we're up in the Tree and the noise don't scare them off? What if they come up after us? How about your slingshot?"

"I don't think so, Rick. I'm not that good with it and it'll be dark. But, hey, that gives me an idea. We were talking about the Tree pods—the prickle pods. I got a sack of them and they're still good and hard and prickly and we've sure had enough practice throwing 'em."

"Oh man, we sure have. We might oughta pick us up some more tonight. Right now I better scoot on home." He starts off, but turns back to his buddy. "You think it'll work? Is it enough? The noise and the prickle pods?"

"Well, it's all we got. Wish we had some firecrackers. Something else, though: we're going to need flashlights, so bring one. And bring anything else you think of. Can you be here by 9:30? I don't think they'll show up 'til they figure there won't be anybody on that road."

"I'll be here, with bells on! Cowbells!"

They go through Lost Lane and part company at the gravel road. Rick is still grinning at his own joke.

Billy walks home, dragging his feet, kicking at gravel. He isn't grinning. His head is churning with the plans. His stomach is churning, too. He's awfully glad to see Punchy sitting on the porch, waiting for him.

CHAPTER SIXTEEN

GULF BREEZE

"**W**hat in all of Nature is this place?" Autumn is looking down at some low buildings near the Gulf, made of weathered gray stone. From the air, she can see they are long and narrow and hooked together in a star shape, with a big space in the middle. Summer doesn't answer until they've landed in that space.

"It's an old fort. Haven't you ever seen one before?" she asks in her irritating what's-the-matter-with-you-Dummy-don't-you-know-anything tone of voice.

"No, I've never seen one. What's a fort?" Autumn's curiosity is stronger than her irritation. Anyway, she's in a much better mood because they've just had a great whoosh to get there. She's seen water, water, water and sparkling white sand and it is all beautiful and the whoosh has cooled her off.

"People fought here a long time ago. That's what Gulf Breeze says. I forget who. They had guns and cannons and cannon balls. You know."

Autumn doesn't know and she would like to, but she guesses she'll ask Gulf Breeze when and if they find him. They make a circuit around the fort. It doesn't take long to spy him sitting in one of the holes in the grey walls, looking out at the water. He doesn't seem all that happy to see his fellow Weatherlings, but when they tell him about the Tree, he agrees to help.

"But we'll need reinforcements," he says.

"Reinforcements?" asks Autumn.

"Yes," he answers, in his confident, lilting voice. "Weatherling reinforcements. I'll get right on it. You two stay here until I get back." And he takes off, trailing a lovely stream of cool air behind him.

"Come on," says Summer. "I'll show you the whole fort." She sounds almost friendly.

CHAPTER SEVENTEEN

GETTING READY

"Hey Pap, can I use your alarm clock tonight to time me on my math problems? We got a timed test coming up next week." Billy and his grandpap have just finished washing and drying the supper dishes.

"You can if I can find it." Pap goes to rummage around in his bedroom. It takes him so long Billy decides he'd better help. He knows that stooping is hard on Pap's back, so he gets down to search the floor and bingo! sees the clock under the chest of drawers.

"Wow, Pap, there's sure been no broom under here for a while. Look at all these dust bunnies." He pulls some out. "Maybe I'll sweep in here tomorrow." He pushes the bunnies back under the chest and wipes his hand on his pants.

The clock is covered with dust and not running, but all it needs is cleaning off and winding up and setting to the right time. Pap says it's about 6:30 but Billy turns on the radio to check. Sure enough, the news is just ending. Pap's inner clock is working fine.

"I got a lot of homework, Pap, so I'll get it done and then get on to bed." As Billy starts for his bedroom, Pap goes over to the big corner cupboard.

"I believe I'm going to have me a drink." He doesn't look at Billy. "I ain't had one all day. Won't hurt to have just a little snort." Billy just nods.

"Goodnight, Pap," he says, "You get a good sleep."

Billy goes into his bedroom to work on the math problems Mr. Sadler has assigned. He's already done his other homework at school, in study hall. That's good because the problems are harder and take more time than he expected. Plus, he has trouble keeping his mind on them. He keeps looking at the clock, worried he'll be late down to the Tree. Punchy seems antsy, too. He sits at the window, looking out, whining every now and then.

"Hey, Punch," Billy whispers, "It'll be okay. By the time I get through with this, Pap'll be asleep and we can gather up what we need and go. You lay down. Be quiet. I can't think."

Punchy stops whining, but stays at the window. It's getting darker out.

Billy forces his mind to go on to the next problem. This one, and two more, and that'll be it. When he finally finishes, he gathers the papers, puts them into his three-ring binder, sighs with relief. "Whew, that was tough."

He has heard Pap getting a second "snort" and then heard him go to bed. That was at 7:45. Pap always leaves his bedroom door open, so Billy hears when the snoring starts just a few minutes later. The whiskey usually makes him go to sleep quicker. And Pap is a sound sleeper.

Homework done, Pap asleep, and time's a'wasting, Billy thinks. "I'm gonna get the stuff now, Punchy. You stay here."

He goes out the back and crawls under the little porch to get a feed sack half-full of the prickle pods that he and Rick throw at trees and fences and stick targets. Sometimes squirrels, but they've never hit one yet. Good practice for baseball—they both want to be pitchers. He also picks up an empty feed sack from the back porch railing, then heads back in to get the flashlight he keeps under his bed, and the clock. An idea strikes him. He gets two pot lids out of the cabinet. He remembers Rick said to bring a whistle. He's got one, on a chain, but he hasn't seen it lately.

Back in the bedroom, he stands at the doorway, and looks around. "Whistle, whistle, where's the whistle, Punchy?" he whispers. He rummages through the top drawer of his dresser, where he puts his comic books and marbles and other stuff. The money he's been saving is there, pushed up in the back corner. He thinks about that gator-handled knife again. No whistle in the drawer. It's not on any of the hooks in the closet. He looks at the clock. Time's running out. Where is the dang thing? He hasn't used it for a long time.

Grandmam always said when you want to find something, stop and think about where you last had it or saw it. Billy knows he took the whistle to a baseball game at school in the spring. His collection of caps are on the bedpost that's up against the corner. He crawls across the bed and finds his New York Yankees cap at the bottom of the stack. Hanging underneath it and to the back of the bedpost, is the whistle. *Thank goodnes*s. Billy puts it around his neck and stuffs the other things into the prickle pod sack.

He looks at the sack and rubs his wristband. "Shoot, Punchy, all I got is a clock and a flashlight and two pot lids and this whistle. And about half a bag of prickle pods. It ain't much." Well, maybe Rick has been able to find more stuff. But what if Rick doesn't show up at all? He will if he can, Billy knows that, but what if something has happened to stop him? Like if his parents have to stay up with a sick cow. "No use standing here worrying about it," he says. "Come on, Punch, let's us get going."

CHAPTER EIGHTEEN

WAITING

It's dark down at the Tree. Not much moon showing and not many stars out yet. Billy takes the noise makers out of the sack. He turns on his flashlight to look around. No sign that anybody has been there. He checks the clock. Too early for Rick.

Using the flashlight, he gathers the hard prickle pods until he's got two feed sacks full of them, puts the sacks under the Tree and feels along the gash again. He's been getting more and more scared, but feeling that gash gets his dander up and anger pushes fear out of the way. He walks on the big limb, climbs a little way and then goes around to the back where the heart is. Grandmam carved that heart. He traces it with his finger. SJB loves AJB. At the same time he remembers the cool air that came from above the day before. The leaves of the Tree enfold him as he leans against the trunk and holds onto his daddy's wristband. He feels comforted. The Tree understands what's going on. He pictures Grandmam smiling at him, and...he thinks something else is nearby, something he can't name and can't see, but it's something friendly. Maybe something that blows cool air.

"Everything's going to be all right," he says to his Tree. He settles down on his branch by the heart to wait for Rick and to think. Punchy jumps onto the walk-up limb and lies there.

When Billy figures it must be getting close to nine o'clock, he climbs down, turns on his flashlight again and checks the clock. Yep, five minutes 'til nine. He's anxious again and sort of sick to his stomach. He leans against the Tree and waits. In a few minutes, Punchy whines and runs over to the Lost Lane bushes.

"Quiet, Punchy. You come back over here. It's got to be Rick, but you be quiet, anyway." Punchy does as he's told. Billy gathers the little dog in his arms and hunkers down behind the Tree. He hears some faint clanking sounds. It's Rick, all right, squeezing out from the bushes, tugging a feed sack behind him. The clanks are coming out of it.

"Hey, Rick, you got here quick. Your folks go to bed early?"

Rick has to catch his breath before he answers. He's run most of the way. "No, it just didn't take me long to gather up the stuff. I knew where everything was."

Billy keeps his voice low. "What all you got in there? You got the cowbells?" Rick nods and grins.

"How'd you keep them from making a racket?"

"Stuffed wash rags in them and wrapped them up in dish towels," says Rick. "But the clock's been knocking up against the tin box. I took Mama's recipes outta there and she'll skin me alive if I don't get that box back with everything put back in it before she gets up tomorrow. It's a good thing she just throws 'em in there. Oh man, she'll write a recipe on anything. I'd hate to have to put that bunch of papers and cards and envelopes back in some kind of order."

"You'll get it home in time. Speaking of that, I don't know how much time we've got right now. We got to figure out our plan."

"I been thinking about it," says Rick. "We ought not be in the same place. Maybe one of us up in the Tree and the other back of those big bushes over there. Not too close to Lost Lane, but close enough so's we can get away if we need to. Oh hey, I brought a sack for prickle pods.

"I already got two sacks full, but we can pick up some more—have a extra bunch stashed somewhere." says Billy. "You know what we might could do? Throw prickle pods at the truck. That'd make some noise and coming from two directions, and all the clocks and stuff, maybe they'll think there's a whole bunch of us here.

"And Rick, I'll be the one in the Tree. I'll get up there now and put my stuff in the hidey hole. I'll hang my prickle pod sack on a branch. You get set up behind the bushes."

"Wait a minute," says Rick. "You got to take a cowbell. Did you bring your whistle? I'll keep the box and both clocks with me. Can you get far enough out on a limb to hit the truck?"

"If they come right up close under the tree again. I won't take a cowbell, though," says Billy. "I brought some lids and I'll need both hands to bang them together. I'll keep my whistle in my mouth." Suddenly he feels, again, like it's hopeless. Two cowbells, two clocks, two whistles, a tin box, two pot lids and a bunch of prickle pods. They must be crazy to think this will work. He sure hopes Fat Man and Pimples don't show up.

Rick's thinking that this is the most exciting thing he's ever done. He turns on his flashlight. "Okay, I'm setting the alarm to the same place on the clocks. When it's time, I'll just turn the hands to the right spot. I can get them going off practically the same time and with 'em sitting on this metal box, it'll be real loud!"

Billy doesn't want to discourage his buddy. "Sounds good, Rick. So...clocks on the box right by you. Whistle in your mouth. Cowbells by the box to pick up when you get the clocks going. Move off a good ways to start the cowbells so it'll seem like at least three of us. Sack of prickle pods nearby for when you're ready to throw. Keep that flashlight pointed to the ground while you get set up, then turn it off and don't use it 'less you have to. And when you hear the truck, be sure it's turned off. That's *if* you hear the truck. They may not show up."

Rick starts over to the bushes, then stops and turns around. "Hey, what about Punchy?"

"Punchy's going to be in Lost Lane. Come on, pal." Billy picks up the little dog, squeezes through the bushes, and puts him down on the lane. "You stay right there. Stay. And quiet, Punchy." He shines the flashlight on his own face and put his finger on his lips.

Punchy doesn't like it. When Billy starts to walk away, Punchy follows.

"No, Punchy. Stay." Billy pushes him back and points his finger at him. Punchy sits. As soon as Billy leaves, he moves through the undergrowth back to the bushes and lies there, hidden, with his muzzle on his paws and his ears pricked up.

Billy and Rick hurry to get into their positions. Then they settle down to wait.

CHAPTER NINETEEN

THE BATTLE AT THE TREE

Punchy hears the truck while it's still a mile away. He's been listening to Rick snoring. He hasn't heard any sounds from the Tree since Billy climbed up there.

The truck is coming fast. Punchy runs out to Rick and nudges his arm. Rick stops snoring, shrugs his arm away and turns over onto his other side. Punchy nudges harder and barks. Rick's eyes open.

"Punchy, what…?" Then he hears the faint sound of the truck. "Oh man, here they come! Here they come!" He turns on his flashlight, points it to the ground, and runs over to the Tree.

"Hey, Billy!"

"I hear you, Rick. Not so loud. Get on back to your spot and get ready. Turn that light off. Punchy, you get back into the bushes. Rick, take him over there and tell him to stay and to be quiet. Say it like you mean it."

Punchy whines, but he goes with Rick and lies down until Rick leaves, then he's up and facing toward the noise of the truck. He stays, though, and he keeps quiet.

Rick's bushes are a good ways in back of the Tree. His heart is pounding. It's not just from excitement now—he's scared. What he most wants is to take off running for Lost Lane. But he can't leave Billy up in the Tree with that pickup coming.

Billy is scared, too, but he's not thinking about running. The whistle chain is around his neck. The pot lids are in Grandmam's hidey hole. He has used the rough end of a broken branch to poke a hole through the top of the sack of prickle pods and it's hanging there on the branch. He's thinking he may throw up.

When Rick's light turns off down below, Billy puts the whistle in his mouth and gets the lids ready to clang. He sits there on his branch, backed up against the tree trunk and rubbing his wristband. It feels like the tree is holding onto him. That calms him down some. He puts his head up against the hidey hole and hears Grandmam's voice, telling him he can do this. Then he feels puffs of cool air on the side of his neck and knows that the Tree Friend is there. He turns his head but sees nothing.

The sound of the pickup gets louder and the boys can see its lights. In just a few minutes, it turns off the road and comes on through the underbrush, dodging trees and running over small bushes and saplings. It stops underneath the mammoth magnolia, about ten feet from the trunk, with headlights shining on it. Fat Man and Pimples climb down out of the truck cab, leaving both doors open. Fat Man is limping a little.

"You shoulda got a bulb for your cab light, Mac. It's too dark out here. We need all the light we can get." Pimples sounds whiny, as usual.

"Didn't get around to it. Headlights ought to be enough, anyway." Fat Man sounds growlier than ever. He looks up at the sky. "Weatherman on the radio said clear tonight, like usual. Ought to be a lot of stars out. Where did all those clouds come from?"

He stretches, then bends over and puts his hands on his knees. "Man, I'm stiff," he says. "That's too long a ride. We should've started earlier and then we could've stopped and got us a burger, 'stead of sitting in this truck for two hours, with nothing but candy bars and Coca Colas. You should've told your mother we didn't have time to get her over to her friend's. Waste of time. Waste of my gas. Oh, but that's right, you don't never worry about wasting my gas."

"Aw Mac, I wish you'd quit harping on that. Come on, let's get going on this thing."

"Yeah, you're in a real big hurry now, ain't you? Well then, you just haul that chain saw over here and get started."

Oh man, thought Rick. *We didn't think about headlights. We need to get them turned off. Billy can't do it. Can I do it?* Oh man! The thought scares him half to death. He knows somebody's got to do it.

Up in the tree, Billy's thinking *Rick's got to get those lights off.* Wondering if Rick is up to it. Or maybe he wouldn't even think about it. Pimples is fiddling with the heavy chain saw, getting it into position against the Tree. Billy feels a shiver. He doesn't know if it's him or his Tree. Maybe both. He hears the chain saw start up and, in just about two minutes, the truck lights go out.

Down below, Rick scurries out of the truck, lopes back around the other side of the tree, to his hiding place. He hasn't just turned the lights off, he's pulled the light knob loose and stuck it in his pocket. As soon as he gets back behind the bushes he starts up the clock alarms, then darts off a ways and starts blowing his whistle and ringing the cowbells. Right on cue, Billy gets his whistle and pot lids going.

When the lights go out, Pimples whirls around to look at the truck. Fat Man jumps out of the way just in time.

"Turn that dang thing off, you fool. You coulda took my arm off."

"Okay! Okay! Hold your horses! I can't see squat out here in this dark." Pimples feels for the switch. Over the buzzing of the saw they hear some kind of racket. "What's that, Mac?"

"Well, if you'd get that durned saw turned off, maybe we could tell." Mac takes a flashlight out of his back pocket and shines a weak beam on the chain saw.

Pimples finds the switch and the saw stops. The sounds are pretty loud. They're coming from up in the Tree and from two places over behind bushes.

Pimples drops the saw and heads for the truck. "We better get out of here. Come on Mac, come on. I hope the battery ain't dead." He gets in the truck cab and reaches for the light knob. "What the devil?" he mutters. Then he yells, "Mac, the light knob's done come off."

"Well, find it. I wanna see what's going on here." Mac is standing still, listening to the noises and turning his flashlight beam, which is getting dimmer, this way and that. "It don't sound like nothing but whistles and cowbells and something banging. Some of it's up in the tree. I think there's some jokers out here yankin' our strings." He starts over in the direction of the bushes, flashing his weak light around.

"Come on out here, you mangy goobers," he yells. Right then, his flashlight gives out. He curses and shakes it, but the light won't come back on.

Pimples is feeling all over the floor of the truck cab for the missing knob. He tries to turn on the lights with his hand, but can't get the little stub to move.

"Can't find the knob and can't get the thing to turn. I need that flashlight, Mac—what did you turn it off for?" He gets out of the truck and comes up behind Mac just as the big man stumbles over a root and goes down on his knees. Pimples can't stop himself. He falls over his uncle. He lands on the ground, too, spread out on his stomach. As he sits up, his foot hits Mac's bad knee.

"You idiot!" Mac hits out with his big hand and slaps him on the leg. Plunking noises start coming from the truck.

"What's that?" Pimples gets up and looks over toward the truck. His eyes have adjusted some but it's awfully dark, with clouds all over the sky now. "I can't see doodley squat."

Rick has come out from the bushes, circled around, and is up against a pine tree, hitting the far side pickup door with prickle pods. He knows he's going to have to run if the guys come after him. He inches his way closer to the Lost Lane bushes. Then he thinks about Billy. Maybe he can draw the guys away, get them to chase after him and give Billy a chance to get down out of the Tree so they can make a run for it.

He goes back behind the bushes where he set up the clocks, still blowing the whistle and ringing both cowbells with one hand, while he pulls the sack of prickle pods along in the other. The clock alarms have run down.

Billy is blowing his whistle and banging his lids. He can hear where the men are, but there are too many branches and leaves between him and them for his prickle pods to find the target.

"Help me up, Sport." Pimples takes hold of Mac under his arms and pulls. The big man gets one foot under him and pushes himself up. He bends over to rub his knees for a minute, then his gravelly voice gets mean: "Now let's us just find out what's going on here."

Keep moving, Rick, thinks Billy. *If you can get them on over here a ways, maybe I can zap them with some pods.* He keeps blowing his whistle, but puts the pot lids back in the hidey hole. He's shaking so hard he has trouble getting the sack off the twig and when it comes free he hits his elbow on another branch. Right smack on the funny bone. He has to wait until the pain and tingling stop. Seems to take forever. He hears Rick moving around down below and Fat Man and Pimples stumbling after him, running into each other and cussing.

Billy stops whistling, but leaves the chain around his neck. He takes the sack of pods and starts crawling farther out. If he can get right above them, he might get some good throws in. He doesn't get that far because the limb gets to bending too much, but he does find a spot where the leaves aren't as thick and he can throw through them. Rick is darting around behind bushes and trees and Fat Man and Pimples are between Billy and Rick. Billy's first prickle pod hits the ground back of Pimples. Pimples turns and looks.

"Must be an old seed pod coming down," he says to Fat Man, but then another one hits nearby, and another and another.

"What, it's raining seed pods? Not hardly. Somebody's up in this here tree pitchin' them things at us," says Fat Man. "You get up there and nab him. I'll take care of this here rabbit in the bushes." When Pimples doesn't move, he gives him a push. "I said go get him."

Billy leans over farther. The whistle chain catches on a twig. He loses his balance. Tries to grab hold of a branch, but can't. He falls down through the Tree, bouncing from branch to branch, and lands on the ground with a thud. When he looks up, Fat Man is right there waiting for him.

"Whooee, looky here, Sport. We done caught ourselves a squirrel."

CHAPTER TWENTY

CAUGHT!

Punchy has been running back and forth, back and forth, behind the Lost Lane bushes. He comes through them just in time to see Billy crashing down through the tree and Fat Man grabbing at him. Punchy goes straight for Fat Man's leg, growling and biting. He only gets a mouthful of pants leg, but the attack takes the big man by surprise and he falls down on his knees.

"Dagnabbit!" he yells. Punchy hangs on. The man swats at him, but can't reach back far enough to get in a good blow.

"Don't you hit him!" yells Billy. He throws himself on Fat Man's back and pounds him on the head with his fists.

Pimples had started his search behind the bushes for the now silent "rabbit," but he runs back, grabs Billy's arms, and twists them behind his back.

"You call off your dog, you hear?"

Billy has no choice. "Punchy, stop! No! No, Punchy!"

Punchy lets go reluctantly. As soon as he does, Fat Man gets him by a hind leg with one hand, pulls him around and closes his other hand on the little dog's muzzle.

"We need us something to put this here little varmint in, Sport."

"The Squirrel's done brought us a feed sack, Mac. That'll do the trick." Still holding the struggling Billy by one arm, Sport picks up the sack, empties out the rest of the seed pods, and throws it over to Fat Man.

"Stop it!" Billy jerks away from Sport and grabs for the sack. Too late. Mac dumps Punchy into it, puts it on the ground, and puts his good knee on it to keep it closed. Billy grabs his leg and tries to move it. Mac's big hand takes hold of Billy's arm, squeezing it tight.

"Okay, Sport," he says. "You get the mutt over to the pickup. Find a piece of rope in my tool box and close up that sack good. I'll hold onto the Squirrel. Hey, while you're in there, look for some pliers; we got to get them lights back on. You're gonna have to help me get up—my knee's hurtin' bad. Then we'll take care of this one. I don't hear the Rabbit anymore. He must have headed for the briar patch." Even with his knee hurting, Fat Man manages a guffaw. Sport doesn't think it's that funny, but he laughs too, glad to hear something pleasant from his partner, for a change.

"You can't leave Punchy in that bag!" yells Billy. "He'll suffocate!" Fat Man forces him down on the ground and, with his arms held tight, Billy can only kick out at air.

"He can breathe," says Pimples. "There's a couple of little holes in it; he's got his nose stuck out of one already. Don't worry, I'll take care of him. He's a feisty little runt, ain't he? I'll bet he's a hunter. I wouldn't mind having me a good squirrel dog. Hear that, Mac, a squirrel dog. Or, at least, a squirrel's dog. Yeah, thanks...Squirrel." He takes the sack with the struggling Punchy over to the back of the truck and holds it with one hand while he rummages around in the tool box with the other.

"I can't see worth a durn, Mac. But here's some pliers. Oh wait, here's a flashlight. Cheez, it ain't workin' neither." He feels around some more. "I can't find no rope, Mac."

"You idiot, forget the rope and use them pliers to get the lights on." Fat Man looks at Billy. "What's your name, Squirrel? You know you're in a heap of trouble, don't you? Attacking us out here like this. Causing me to hurt my knee. What are you up to?" He gives Billy a good shake. Billy doesn't say a word.

Pimples is holding the sack with Punchy in it in his left hand. With the pliers in his right hand, he manages to turn the little stub. The headlights come back on.

"I'll look for rope again but I don't think there is any. Would it be somewhere else, Mac?"

"Use your belt."

"I ain't got on a belt. You got on a belt?"

Fat Man looks at him. "You are one useless…" He stops, shakes his head. "Yeah, I got on a belt. My hands are full of Squirrel. You'll have to get it off of me."

Pimples has some trouble getting to the belt, with Fat Man's belly hanging over it, and by the time he's got it unbuckled and out from the loops, Fat Man is cussing at him, and calling him a dope and a big lug and, what seems to be his favorite, an idiot. Pimples sits down and holds the sack between his knees to keep Punchy from wriggling so hard. He uses the pliers to jab two holes on each side of the top of the sack. He threads the belt through them, then winds it tight around the top of the bag, keeping the first belt hole and the buckle clear so he can fasten them together.

"Look at that, Mac. He ain't going to get out of that. That's a good job, ain't it, Mac?"

"Yeah, okay, now get me up from here."

"Well, that's going to be hard to do, what with you havin' to hold onto the Squirrel."

"You're right about that. We need us some duct tape. I know there's some of that in the toolbox, if you ain't too blind to find it. Throw that sack of dog over in the back of the truck. And hurry up. It feels like a storm's coming in."

Billy had not noticed that. Now he becomes aware of the wind. It has sprung up out of nowhere and even as he feels it, it gets stronger. It's not supposed to rain; the guy on the radio had said clear and hot, as usual. Well, it's plenty hot but it isn't clear. The sky is totally covered with clouds and that wind just doesn't feel right.

For one thing, it's coming from the wrong direction. Storms don't usually come from the northeast, do they? They come from the south or the west.

Suddenly rain starts pouring down.

CHAPTER TWENTY-ONE

STORM

"**G**ood gosh a'mighty!" yells Fat Man. "Get me up from here, Sport, I'm gettin' soaked! I got to get in the truck." He shoves Billy away from him, hard. Billy lands against the Tree and falls to the ground with his left foot twisted under him. A sharp pain sears his ankle. He feels the hair stand up on his arms as lightning hits nearby in the woods. Everything lights up. The thunder that follows is deafening.

"Whooee, that was close!" yells Pimples. "Let's get out of here. That wind is something! And, boy, this rain—we got us a gullywasher!" He runs over to help Fat Man just as the big guy gives a push and comes up fast. He bumps into Pimples. Pimples goes down. Fat Man pulls him back up. They hold onto each other and, keeping their heads ducked, make for the truck. They manage to struggle into it. Another close bolt of lightning hits.

"Shut that door quick and roll the window up, Sport," Fat Man orders. Thunder is booming all around. He tries to close the driver's door. The wind is too strong. But Pimples gets his door closed and the window up.

Fat Man starts the motor and turns on the windshield wipers. "I'll move us around to where the wind'll shut this door." But when he gets the truck turned, the wind shifts and comes from the other way. His door still won't close.

"Dang it to all get out!" yells Fat Man. "We got to get away from this mess!" He guns the motor and sets off for the road. With the rain pouring down, he can't see much even with the headlights back on and the wipers going fast. But he's able to feel when the tires reach the pavement.

The wind gets even stronger and rain is coming down in sheets. It's hard to keep the pickup on the road. They get about half a mile from the tree, with the driver-side door still wide open and the pickup careening this way and that. Fat Man is tired of wrestling with it. He slams on the brakes and the truck slides around sideways.

"We gotta get this door shut, Sport. It's too hard to steer." They get out into the drenching rain, the big man wincing with pain at every step. The wind seems to be coming from every direction. They push with all their might on the pickup door.

"It ain't gonna close, I think it's broke." Pimples gets back in the truck. "Geez, I ain't never been this soaked. We'll have to stay here 'til the storm quits."

Fat Man nods, "You're right. It's too much for me." He gets back in, closes his eyes and sits there rubbing his knee. Pimples is looking out his window.

"Hey, Mac, the wind just stopped."

Fat Man opens his eyes. "What? How about that! The rain's lettin' up, too." He pulls on his door. "It'll come around now, but it's bent. We'll have to duct tape it shut. Get back there and find that tape."

"What about the boy? You think we oughta do something about him?"

"Oh, dang, I forgot about the Squirrel. He's probably high-tailed it for home. Who the heck is he, anyway? And the Rabbit." He thinks about it for a moment. "Just kids. Country yokels playing jokes, I'd guess. Well, we taught 'em a lesson. And hey, I just might have got me a feisty little huntin' dog out of the deal, Sport."

"That's my dog, Mac. I claimed him first. Oh hey, he may be drowned back there! I better see." He jumps out of the truck to check on Punchy. What he sees is a very wet, lumpy feed sack smack up against the front corner of the truck bed. It is perfectly still.

CHAPTER TWENTY-TWO

THE RABBIT

The sound of Billy falling down through the tree stops Rick in his tracks. He has been blowing his whistle and ringing the cowbells and running back and forth behind the thick bushes. "Oh man, oh man, don't let them get him," he whispers to himself. He wants to yell, "Run Billy, run," but thinks he'd better not. When he hears Fat Man say they've caught themselves a squirrel, he drops down on the ground and gets quiet.

He hears Punchy attack, hears Billy call him off, hears Fat Man say he's putting Punchy in a sack. Rick doesn't know whether to stay and try to do something or run for help. He tries to decide while Pimples is fastening up the sack, but he's too scared to move.

Hearing Fat Man tell Pimples to get duct tape makes the decision for him. He drops the cowbells and sack and picks up a branch to use as a weapon, but right then it starts raining hard and the wind is so strong he can barely stand up. He crawls up against the Tree and peeks around just as Fat Man shoves Billy away and comes up off the ground. Lightning strikes. Thunder crashes. Rick hears Pimples yell they got to get.

Rick stays where he is. He watches them get into the truck. More lightning lights up everything. Those two sure do want out of there. He doesn't blame them. It scares the dickens out of him, too. More lightning flashes. The thunder rolls on and on.

He watches the men wrestle with the doors of the truck and Pimples get his door closed, but Fat Man doesn't have any luck with his. He sees them drive off, the pickup weaving all over the place. There is so much lightning he can see when they stop, wrestle with the door some more, then get back in the truck.

Rick's got to see if Billy's all right. Maybe he should wait; what if they come back? He doesn't know what to do. Then the wind stops. Just like that. And it's not raining so hard. He hears the truck start up the road again. As he runs to his pal, the rain stops completely. He grabs Billy's arm and shakes it. "Are you okay, buddy?"

"They took Punchy," Billy says. And bursts into tears.

CHAPTER TWENTY-THREE

AFTER THE STORM

As the battered pickup truck weaves its way along the road, Autumn, Summer and Gulf Breeze are sitting at the top of a tall pine tree, watching.

"How in the name of All Nature did you do that?" Autumn asks Gulf Breeze.

"Didn't I tell you he'd do something?" Summer is beaming. She has her know-it-all voice on again. It doesn't even irritate Autumn because she's so happy her Tree is safe.

Gulf Breeze, who is never modest, looks even more pleased with himself now. He's humming and swaying. He doesn't answer.

Autumn keeps after him. "I know you had help. It happened fast, but I saw East Wind and West Wind in the middle of everything, blowing at each other. And I'm pretty sure you couldn't have done that lightning by yourself. Oh, that was magnificent! It was absolutely the brightest lightning and the loudest, longest thunder ever. Those tree-hurters couldn't wait to get out of here. Gulf Breeze, you are a genius."

Gulf Breeze stops humming and smiles at her. For the first time ever. "There were plenty of Weatherlings helping," he says.

Summer notices the smile. She looks over at Autumn and her voice is not friendly. "Don't take it personally. He'd do it for anybody. It doesn't mean we're going to have anything else to do with you. Come on, GB, let's get out of here. The Tree is okay now."

But Gulf Breeze isn't listening to her. He slides down the pine and sees Rick bending over Billy. "I think something's happened to that boy," he says.

They come up close just in time to hear Billy say, "They took Punchy," and start crying.

"Oh, man!" Rick covers his own eyes. "Oh, Man!"

Billy doesn't say anything more for a moment. He looks away and wipes off his tears. "We'll get him back," he says. Rick hopes he's right, but something else is worrying Rick. He has seen Billy wince when he moves his legs.

"Are you hurt, Bill?"

Billy sits up straighter and runs a hand down his left leg to his foot. "It's my ankle. It's swelled up, either sprained or broke, I reckon. You'll have to help me get up, Rick."

Rick feels the puffy ankle, then turns to look around. He can see fine now. The clouds are gone and the moon is up there and stars are shining all over the sky.

He takes both of Billy's hands and pulls. Billy puts weight on his left foot. "Ouch! Yeah, that ankle's bad." Autumn, who has come up close, blows a little cool air on the wet sock covering the puffed up ankle, then blows some on Billy's forehead. She feels like she may cry.

She must look that way, too, because Summer pokes her in the side, and hisses "Silly Seedling!" which doesn't help. Gulf Breeze bends down and blows a big stream of cool on the ankle. Billy holds up his hand to see where the air is coming from. His ankle feels a little better. He feels a little better himself—his Tree Friend is here.

"You think maybe it's just a sprain? If it's a break, you don't want to be walking on it," warns Rick.

"I don't know which it is. But either way, I can't walk on it. Get me some kind of branch to lean on."

This is one way Autumn can help. She whooshes over to Lost Lane and finds a fallen oak branch that looks about the right size, strips off the few leaves that are on it, and smooths off the two ends with her strong fingernails. Then she upstretches to pull down some Spanish moss that's hanging in a long, tangled, gray beard from an oak branch. It'll make a cushion for Billy's underarm.

Rick is scrabbling around, looking on the ground near the Tree, but isn't finding a branch that will fit Billy, when something hits the ground behind him.

"Hey Bill, here's one just dropped from the Tree. It ain't a magnolia branch; musta been blown up there by all that wind. There's Spanish moss on it. We'll use that on the top so you can put it under your arm. I wish we had my crutches here. The ones I used after I had polio. They're stored up in the hayloft. I'll bring 'em to you tomorrow."

"Rick, you're a genius. Let's get going. No, wait. We got to take back the stuff we brought out here. You still got a sack? Don't worry about the lids. They're okay in the hidey hole. Hey, what about that chain saw? We can't leave it out here to rust. That storm's soaked everything! And we sure don't want those guys coming back and finding it."

By the time Rick has gathered up the noise makers, the sun is coming up. "Geez, Billy, it's morning already." He still has the whistle around his neck, but Billy's is gone. Rick can't manage the heavy chain saw, what with so much stuff in the bag and Billy having to lean on him.

"We'll have to leave the saw in Lost Lane," Rick says. He dumps out the rest of his prickle pods and puts the saw into his sack. Both the saw and the sack are, surprisingly, dry. He drags it through the bushes and into the lane, and covers it with leaves. Golly, the leaves are dry, too. He forgets about all that, though, when he goes back for Billy.

"Rick, Pap's probably going to be awake by the time we get there and your folks are going to be up, for sure. We'll have to tell 'em something. I don't think we can say anything about those guys yet. Not when it looks like Pap's the one that hired them. We have to decide what we can tell. Without lying, if we can help it. Pap'll catch me in a lie every time."

"I don't lie unless I just can't get out of it," Rick says. "I don't see how we can get out of it now." He helps Billy get through the bushes. He shows him where he's hidden the chain saw. They start up Lost Lane. Billy has his left arm over Rick's right shoulder and the Spanish moss-padded branch under his right arm. Rick drags the clanking sack with his left hand. Neither of them says anything about Punchy.

Autumn, Summer and Gulf Breeze watch them go. They don't say anything about Punchy, either, but each one is thinking about him. Then Summer blows hot air in Autumn's face and takes hold of Gulf Breeze's arm. "Let's get out of here, partner. The Tree's safe. I don't think those two Nature butchers are going to show up here again after what you did to them."

Gulf Breeze shrugs away from her grasp. "I don't know. They may come back for their saw. And I'm afraid those boys are going to be in a mountain of trouble when they get home."

"I know where Billy lives," says Autumn. "We can whoosh over and be there when he gets home. See what happens."

Summer shakes her head, but when Gulf Breeze says, "Okay, let's whoosh," she whooshes right along with them.

CHAPTER TWENTY-FOUR

SAFE AT HOME

"What in tarnation...? Billy Boy?"

Pap is standing on the porch steps with a coffee mug in his hand when the boys come hobbling up the road. He looks back, then at the boys, and comes down the steps to meet them.

"Your door's closed and I thought you was still in bed. I just woke up. Here, Rick, you let me have him. What happened? Where you two been? You look like you've been run through a sheep wash." He puts his arm around Billy's waist.

"I'm okay Pap. I'll tell you about it, but Rick's got to get home. You go on, buddy. Thanks. Thanks a lot."

Rick takes off as fast as he can go, dragging the clanking sack behind him, looking back to call, "I'll bring you those crutches."

"Let's get you up here on a chair, boy. That ankle's all swole up." Pap puts his mug down, pitches the makeshift crutch under the porch and helps Billy hop on his good leg up the steps to Grandmam's rocker. It had been rocking gently but now it's still.

"I'm glad you ain't been sitting here worrying about me," says Billy. "I'm sorry, Pap. Rick and me decided to spend the night at the Tree and a big old storm came up and...."

Pap interrupts him. "No, you tell me later. Let me get a look at this ankle. Be still, I got to get your shoe and sock off." The shoe comes off okay after he unlaces it, but he uses his pocket knife to cut the wet, clinging, sock. Billy's ankle looks big as a softball.

"Whoo, that's a beauty, boy." Very gently, he turns Billy's foot this way and that, his fingers probing the ankle and foot. Billy shuts his eyes tight and screws up his face.

"That hurts, don't it," Pap says. "Well, nothing's broke. Feels like it's just a bad sprain. But we got to do something about it. You ain't going to school today, that's for sure. Let's get you into the house and out of these wet clothes."

He picks up Billy and carries him in. Autumn, who had moved from Grandmam's rocker to Pap's, gets up to follow.

"Comets and Stars! Give the boy some privacy." Summer, who has been unusually quiet since they left the Tree, seems to have found her normal order-giving voice again.

"I want to hear what he tells Pap," Autumn retorts. "But you're right, maybe we ought to stay outside. How about if we go around to the back porch and just listen?" Since the others are as curious as she is, that's what they do. Autumn and Summer sit with their backs up against the screen door, each making it very obvious that she's not looking in. Gulf Breeze perches on a short stool over by the rail. He says he can hear fine from there.

In a few minutes, Pap carries Billy, who's now mostly dry and wearing big-legged, short-sleeved pajamas, into the kitchen. He sits him down on a chair at the table. "Give me a minute here to heat up some water, Billy Boy. Durned old water heater's not gettin' it hot enough. I expect you're hungry, ain't you?" He fills a big kettle and puts it on the stove burner, then gets bacon out of the refrigerator and starts frying it in the skillet. He pours another mugful of coffee for himself and one for his grandson. He stirs milk and sugar into Billy's. It's about the best coffee Billy has ever smelled or tasted.

"Okay now, boy, let's hear it."

Billy starts talking: He and Rick had wanted to spend part of the night at the tree. They were afraid Rick's parents and Pap might not let them if they asked. They meant to be back way before dawn.

But a big storm came up with a lot of rain and lightning and Billy fell out of the Tree and his ankle got hurt. It's all true, he's just left out a lot. He waits to hear what Pap says.

Pap flips the bacon slices and turns down the burner. He gulps some coffee and says, "I wish we had us some more biscuits. Nothin' like biscuits to stick to your ribs. But I'll fry up eggs and there's plenty of bacon." That makes him think of somebody else who likes bacon. He looks around. "Where's Punchy?"

That's the question Billy's been dreading. He looks at his coffee mug as he answers. "After the storm, he disappeared." That was the truth.

"That ain't like Punchy, to run off and leave you," Pap says. "And he ain't usually scared of storms." That makes him think of something else. "How bad was it? I don't see no sign of a storm here."

And that's the first time Billy realizes that when they came back through Lost Lane, and all the way home, nothing was wet. How could such a storm have stopped right at Lost Lane? He shakes his head. He doesn't know how to answer.

"Billy Boy? How bad was that storm? I didn't hear nothing." Pap raises his voice a little, thinking Billy hasn't heard him. Or maybe he's just too tired to talk. Still, Pap wants to know about that storm. If it was so close by and there was thunder and lightning, he should have waked up. Just how much whiskey had he drank last night? Too much to rouse up if something happened to the house? To Billy Boy?

"It was pretty bad," Billy says. "I'm surprised you didn't hear the thunder. But I guess the rain didn't make it this far."

Pap doesn't say anything for a while. He breaks eggs into a bowl. Every now and then he puts his hands on his hips and bends over. His back is bothering him bad from picking up his grandson.

When the water in the kettle comes almost to a boil, Pap pours it into a big bucket and adds cold water, testing it with his elbow until it's the right temperature. He stirs some Epsom Salts in with a long wooden spoon, then sets the bucket by Billy. He kneels down slowly and rolls Billy's pajama leg up, then picks up the hurt foot and puts it in the water.

"How does that feel? Them salts is gonna help take that swelling down."

"It feels about right. Thanks, Pap." Billy reaches over with both arms and hugs his grandfather. Pap hugs him back, turning his head away. He holds on to the table to raise himself up, wipes his sleeve across his face, and gets busy at the stove.

"Dadgummit, I've let the bacon burn." He picks up a piece with a fork and looks at both sides. "Well, not too bad, we can still eat it. I'll fix those eggs and we'll have us a good breakfast. Let's open that jar of fig preserves Miz Garraway gave us a while back. They'll make this old store-boughten bread taste a whole heap better."

Out on the back porch, Autumn and Summer have been sneaking peeks into the kitchen. Now they look at each other. "He's not a bad old man," says Autumn. "He loves the boy, you can tell he does. I wonder why the boy doesn't tell him what happened? Pap knows those tree cutters. He can get the dog back."

"Maybe he can, maybe he can't," Summer says. "Can't you do something about Punchy, GB?"

Gulf Breeze is looking at the back yard. "We don't know where those guys went. No, nothing I can do about it." His voice is as clear and cool as ever, but it's not as happy. Autumn thinks he must be pretty upset. She suspects that Summer is, also, though she'd probably never admit it. Well, the boy is safe; both boys are safe. Thanks to All Good Nature for that.

Inside the house, Pap pulls the table closer to Billy and sets the food on it. His back twinges and he rubs it, then pours more coffee for his grandson.

Billy is happy to get it—Pap usually just gives him one mugful. He takes a big swallow. He's nice and dry now. But with his foot in the water, he's getting awful hot. He pulls the other pajama leg up above his knee and unbuttons the pajama top. Then he sets in to eat his breakfast. Pap gets himself some and sits at the table, eating and looking out the back screen door. He's wondering about that storm. Wondering about a lot of things. He doesn't feel like Billy has told him the whole story. He finishes his bacon and eggs, then pushes his chair back from the table. Doesn't say a word, doesn't even look at Billy. Just sits there, drinking his coffee and waiting.

Billy wipes up his last bit of egg with his last bit of bread and eats it. He takes a final gulp of coffee, then looks his grandpap square in the face.

"Pap," he says, "two guys took Punchy."

CHAPTER TWENTY-FIVE

TALKING TO PAP

"Two guys took Punchy? What are you talking about, Billy Boy?"

"Two guys in an old pickup. They came right up to the Tree real late. I was in the Tree and Rick was down on the ground with Punchy and they drove up and we hid to see what they were going to do. Well, they were down there getting things out of the truck and I fell out of the tree and one of them grabbed me. Punchy charged, got one of 'em by the pants leg. Rick was running around trying to get them to chase him and leave me alone. Then it started to storm something fierce and the biggest guy shoved me down and they grabbed Punchy and put him in a feed sack and drove off with him tied up in that sack in the back of the pickup, in the rain. When I tried to stand up, my ankle hurt, so Rick fixed me a crutch and helped me home."

Billy thinks maybe that's all he'd better say. He sits back in his chair and waits.

Pap hasn't said a word the whole time. But Pap's face is red.

"Them two shoved you down?"

Billy nods. "One of them did."

"Them two took Punchy?"

Billy nods again. Pap pushes up from his chair, goes to look out the window, rubs his back and bends over again to try and stretch it out.

Billy slumps down in the chair. His grandfather looks back at him. What a pitiful sight. Hair all matted, eyes red and squinched up, skinny body looking so small in those baggy pajamas. *The boy is plumb wore out,* Pap thinks. *Can't hardly keep his eyes open.* Pap kneels down and takes Billy's foot out of the bucket of water, dries it off with a dish towel, and pulls both pajama legs down. He has trouble getting himself back up from the floor, but he still picks up his grandson to carry him to bed.

Billy nestles up against Pap's bony chest, breathing in the warm, sweaty smell of his work shirt and overalls. Pap eases him down onto the bed and Billy turns on his right side, snuggles his head into the pillow, and starts breathing slow and easy.

Pap stands there for a moment, looking at his grandson. He rubs his back some more. He's sure done something to it, lifting Billy Boy around like that. He thinks about Mac Albert and that greasy kid. He thinks about Punchy. His face gets all red again. He has to make a phone call.

CHAPTER TWENTY-SIX

PHONE CALL

Pap picks up the phone and is relieved there's nobody on it. He's got a four-party line, but the other folks are usually too busy this early in the morning to be making calls. Allie Burnette's phone rings ten times before she answers and Pap gets more anxious with every ring. He's afraid he won't be able to get hold of her and he's nervous and he's mad. Mostly mad. He doesn't know who he's maddest at: her, them two losers, or himself.

"What took you so long?" he asks, when she finally picks up and says hello.

"Sorry, I was in the bathtub. You don't sound so good, Pap. Are you okay? Is Billy Boy okay?"

"I'm fine and he's okay. He's hurt his ankle, but he's okay. I got to talk to you about that guy you sent here. Mac Albert. It's turned into a mess. He brought his nephew in on the deal with him, and the two of them have turned out to be bad news and...."

Allie interrupts. "What's wrong with Billy Boy's ankle?"

"It's sprained, just sprained. It's them guys I got to talk to you about."

"You think you need to take him to the doctor?"

"No he don't need no doctor. I've seen a heap of sprains in my life. I'm tending to it."

"Yeah, okay. I know you'll take good care of him. But you take him to the doctor if it doesn't get better." There's a pause, then she goes on. "Well, about Mac Albert, I just did what you asked me to,

Pap. You said you wanted somebody to kill that tree and Mac was willing to do it. I guess he needed some help, that tree's huge. What nephew did he bring?"

"Young pimple-faced twerp. Called him Sport. Not the brightest bulb, I can tell you that, and I only seen him once. But now, here's the situation. They been down to the tree but some things happened and they've botched the job, and they've run off with Billy Boy's dog."

"Punchy? What would they want him for?"

"I don't know, but you know Billy Boy thinks the world of that dog. You got to talk to Mac and get him back. I don't know how to get a hold of the guy. Just exactly where is he?"

"You told me you didn't want to know anything about him, didn't want any contact with him except to set up the job and then pay him off when it was done. And I told him that's how it was going to be and he said that was fine. I've known him since high school. He's not much, but he'll finish the job, because he needs the money. He's too lazy to get steady work. And you said all he has to do is cut into the tree six inches all the way around."

"Well, this here's something different from the job. He had no call to take our boy's dog. I want to know where he is."

"He's living in a cabin in that old fish camp north of town, near the river. You remember Catfish Cabins? You went up there fishing with us a few times."

"Yeah, I remember Catfish Cabins. You need to get yourself there and get the dog. Right now."

There's a silence on the other end of the line. Pap fidgets with the phone cord, getting more and more agitated.

"Okay, here's the way it is, Pap. It's six thirty now and I've got to be at the cafe in thirty minutes. I don't get off until nine thirty tonight and I'll be worn out, being on my feet all day. It's the same thing all week 'cause we got a girl out sick. I won't have any time off until Saturday afternoon."

"Nine thirty every night? Well, I sure hope you're gettin' paid overtime. Okay then, how about calling Mac Albert?"

"Can't. The cabins aren't hooked up to the phone line. There's one in a booth at the entrance, but somebody has to be near it to hear it ring. Anyway, I wouldn't want to leave a message with anybody about this. And I'm not going to use the gas and time to go find out he's not even there. That camp's way up the highway.

"I tell you what, though, Pap: he works some Saturdays down the street at Western Auto. When they need extra muscle for a tire shipment or something. I'll call first thing Saturday morning and if he's there I'll go over and see him. Or he may come into the cafe before then."

"Wrestlin' tires at Western Auto. That's about all he'd be good for, all right. And just some weekends, not every weekend? So maybe you will and maybe you won't get ahold of him Saturday."

"Well, if that doesn't work, I'll go to the cabin Saturday afternoon. I guess I could leave a note on his door if he's not there."

Pap isn't happy with the idea of waiting so long. "What am I supposed to tell Billy Boy?"

"Well, if you're in such a durned hurry, why don't you just drive up here and get the dog yourself?"

"Don't think I wouldn't if I could. Thing is, I've put my back out again. I can hardly sit down, let alone drive a car for two hours or so. Old car wouldn't make it, anyway. No, you need to do something yourself, but you need to do it quick."

"Well I've told you why I can't do anything any quicker. Were you even listening? And don't you dare tell Billy Boy anything about me being in on this," says Allie. "I'm not having him thinking it's something I'm to blame for. Just tell him it'll take a few days but you'll get the dog for him. Drat that dog. Drat Mac. What would he do a stupid thing like that for?"

"Because he's stupid, Allie," says Pap.

Billy had been almost asleep when Pap put him in bed. But just after Pap goes out of the room and closes the door, a sharp pain in the hurt ankle jars him awake. He reaches down to rub it and looks at Punchy's blanket lying there by the bed. Then he hears Pap in the kitchen, dialing the phone. The phone is on the wall between the kitchen and Billy's room. Pap hardly ever makes calls. Billy gets out of bed and crawls over to the door. It doesn't quite fit at the top or at the bottom, so even though Pap is talking low, Billy can hear every word.

From the beginning of the call, when Pap has to answer questions about the ankle, Billy suspects that he knows who Pap is talking to, but he isn't sure until the very end, when Pap says her name. Allie. His own mama. She's the one who sent Fat Man and Pimples.

Billy gets back into bed with his mind made up. Now he knows where to find Fat Man. He's going to Crowley tomorrow. He's not coming back without Punchy.

CHAPTER TWENTY-SEVEN

PLANNING A TRIP

After Pap finishes his phone call, he cleans up the breakfast dishes. Then he quietly opens the door to Billy's room. Billy is sound asleep. Pap rummages around in the kitchen until he finds an old, flat rubber bag that can be used for an ice pack or a hot water pack. He gets an ice tray from the little freezer at the top of the refrigerator. He pulls the lever over to loosen the ice, fills the bag halfway and screws on the little round top. He wraps a towel around it so it won't be too cold and uses another to keep it wrapped around Billy's ankle. Billy doesn't stir when Pap gently puts it in place. Pap stays in the house so he can hear if Billy wakes up.

Billy sleeps most of the rest of Tuesday. When he stirs, his grandpap puts more ice in the rubber bag and tells him to go back to sleep. Each time he wakes, Billy thinks about Punchy and worries about how he's going to get to Crowley to find him, but he can't stay awake long enough to figure it out.

He's worried about Rick, too. Afraid that his parents were hard on him when he got home. Afraid that Rick was out in that rain too long and caught a cold or something. He wishes Rick would bring those crutches so he'd know his friend is all right, but if he is all right, he's probably gone to school.

The swelling in the ankle goes down steadily, but Pap won't let him get up for anything except to go to the bathroom. He helps Billy hop there so he doesn't put weight on his left foot. By suppertime, it's looking a lot better and Pap helps him into the kitchen to eat. Something sure smells good.

"Hey, roast beef! We don't hardly ever have a roast, Pap." Billy cuts off a piece and stuffs it in his mouth. It's kind of dry, but he's so hungry it tastes fine. "Mmm, this is good." He takes a bite of mashed potatoes. They're a little lumpy and he puts butter on them and mashes it around with his fork. "Good potatoes, too," he says, with his mouth full.

Pap ducks his head. "I didn't cook the roast. It's some Miz Garraway brought us a while back. It was way too much, but she said to freeze some of it. All I did was thaw it and heat it up. It'll give you some energy. You slept just about all day."

"Well, I'm finally awake and my ankle's good as new. Maybe I'll go see Rick after we do the dishes. See how he's doing." Billy now has a plan.

"Naw boy, you ain't going nowhere nor washing no dishes, neither. That ankle's not good as new, not by a long shot."

Billy has to see Rick. For one thing, he needs those crutches tonight if he's going to get to Crowley the next day. He doesn't want to disobey Pap, but if Rick doesn't show up before dark, well, he'll just have to wait until Pap goes to sleep and go down to the Showers' house.

It turns out he doesn't need to do that. Around 6:30, Rick pops in the front door with a plate of gingerbread in his hands and the crutches hanging from his shoulders. Pap's clock is tucked under his arm. He puts the crutches and the clock on the sofa and the three of them sit around the table with milk and gingerbread. Rick says his folks were so glad he was okay, they didn't punish him. His dad gave him a good talking to, though. His mama made breakfast for him, then he cleaned up and went to school. He'd had a lot of trouble staying awake.

Nobody mentions the clock.

Rick asks about Billy's ankle and Billy holds it up for him to see and the three talk mostly about the ankle and the gingerbread and what happened at school that day. Those are topics that seem safe.

Pap is tired and his back is hurting worse. He needs to sit in his big chair and put his feet up on the ottoman and stretch out and have a little snort of whisky. But he doesn't want to drink in front of Rick.

"How's about you boys sittin' on the porch so's I can listen to the radio? Help him out there, Rick. Oh, and you tell your mama the gingerbread was mighty fine. And tell her and your daddy thanks for lending Billy Boy them crutches."

"I will, Mr. Burnette. Come on, Bill, let's get these fixed up to fit you."

Rick helps his friend hop out and onto the porch steps, then goes back in and brings the crutches and the empty gingerbread plate. Billy has scooted down to the lowest step where they'll have more privacy. Each takes a crutch, loosens the screws, and pulls it out longer to fit Billy. They don't talk about anything but the crutches until they're done. By then, the radio is on, playing country music, and Pap is snoring, so Billy gets started.

"Rick, I got to go to Crowley tomorrow. That's where they've got Punchy."

"Oh man! How'd you find out?"

Billy doesn't tell Rick about his mama being involved. "I heard Pap talking on the phone to somebody that lives there and knows where Fat Man lives and I'll bet you anything he's the one that kept Punchy. If he didn't, he'll know where he is."

"How you going to get up there? That's at least two hours driving. Your grandpap going to take you?"

"Pap don't know that I know. I heard him talking on the phone after I went to bed this morning."

"Well, what about your mama? Don't she live up there? She could come get you, maybe. Or pick up Punchy and bring him home."

"It's hard for Mama to get off work. Anyhow, I don't want to worry her with this. I can handle it myself."

Rick knows that Billy's mama sends money but doesn't come see him much and he wonders if it bothers Billy. He drops that subject.

"So what are you going to do?" he asks.

"I'm going to start off like I'm going to school, then cut through the pasture and the woods and head up to Crenshaw's Corner— that's not too far, with the crutches— and take the Greyhound bus. Grandmam and I did that one time when we went to see Mama. The bus picks people up at the Corner around eight thirty. It'll stop a few other places, if there's anybody out waiting for it, but it'll get to Crowley around eleven thirty or so. Then I'm going to find Fat Man. I heard Pap say his name—it's Mac Albert—and I heard where he lives and where he works sometimes."

"Oh man! You got money for the bus?"

"Yeah, I got six dollars and fifty four cents that I've been saving for a new bike. And I'll take my lunch. We had roast tonight and there's enough left for sandwiches. You tell people my ankle's still bothering me. That's true, but it's not bothering me enough to keep me from finding Punchy. Oh, and another thing, I want you to take my homework in for me. It's already a day late."

Rick starts to say something, but Billy stops him. "Here's something else, Rick. I don't know when I'll get back or be able to phone, and I don't want Pap to worry. So I'm going to write him a note and leave it under my pillow. I want you to come by after school, as late as you can, but before he has time to get worried. He'll think I've stopped at your house but he'll expect me home before supper time. You act surprised that I'm not here, tell him I wasn't at school, but that you just figured my ankle was still too bad. When he starts to get upset, tell him you'll look around and see if you can figure out where I might be. Go in my bedroom and find the note under the pillow. It'll say where I went and what for and that I'll be in touch with Mama up there."

"What if he finds the note before I get there?"

"He won't. I always spread up my bed and he's got no reason to bother it. Anyway, his back's hurting him and he's not going to be moving around much."

"Man, I sure wish I could go with you."

"I sure wish you could, too, Rick."

CHAPTER TWENTY-EIGHT

HEAT DAMAGE

When the listeners on the back porch hear Billy say, "Pap, two guys took Punchy," Gulf Breeze stands up and starts down the steps. "Come on, let's go. It's up to them to find the dog. We've got other things to think about."

Summer is at his side like a flash of lightning.

Autumn wants to stay and hear what Pap has to say, but she knows if she lets them out of her sight, she might not find them again. She catches up at the front yard and both of them stop.

"Where do you think *you're* going?" Summer is very unfriendly again.

Autumn talks fast. "I want to thank you two. You ran off those tree butchers and saved the Tree." She doesn't really think Summer has done anything, but figures she'd better include her. "I don't know what would have happened if it hadn't been for you. Maybe I can help you sometime. I hope so. Weatherlings need to stick together."

She doesn't like the look Summer's giving her, and Gulf Breeze is wandering around like he isn't even listening.

"You can help us right now," said Summer. "You can help us by skydoodling out of here. Go back to where you came from. This is our territory and we don't want you here. *Nobody* wants you here. Isn't that right, GB?"

"I don't know," says the cool voice. He's looking at a pine tree in the side yard. "I'm thinking all this heat going on for so long isn't good for the Greenstuff. Look how dry everything is."

"What are you talking about? The Greenstuff's fine. Just look at this nice persimmon tree." Summer waves them over and all three peer at the tree. Gulf Breeze reaches out and breaks off a leaf and it crumbles in his fingers. The Weatherlings move around the yard, examining the other trees and bushes.

Autumn starts to say, "He's right," but decides against it. If there's one thing she knows about Summer, it's that she's likely to disagree with anything Autumn says. But since Summer thinks Gulf Breeze knows everything she might listen to him. Autumn moves away from them to a thick-trunked, brown wisteria vine. She doesn't go far, though, and she can tell they're arguing, even though she can't hear every word.

"Well, you may be right, but I'm not leaving here." Summer says that clearly. Her voice grows louder. "I like it here. I'd like it to be even hotter here. The Greenstuff will adjust."

Gulf Breeze's voice is as cool as ever, but low, and Autumn can't make out his answer. When he calls out, "Come on, Autumn," she rejoins them. Summer is looking at the ground. Gulf Breeze is looking at the tree tops. Without another word, the three whoosh themselves up and over the trees and are soon in the shelter of the Underpier at the beach.

They sit quietly. Each Weatherling is thinking about the dry, brown, Greenstuff.

CHAPTER TWENTY-NINE

CROWLEY

Wednesday morning goes just like Billy has planned. He thought there might be somebody on the bus who would know him and he was all set to say he was going to see his mother, but they're all strangers. He's glad to get a window seat. He left one of the crutches, covered up by leaves, under a small magnolia tree at the edge of the woods across from Crenshaw's Corner. It was too hard to use both of them and hold onto a lunch sack.

The man who sits down by him glances at his crutch but just nods hello and starts reading his newspaper. Billy rubs his wristband and worries about Punchy while he looks out at fields, pecan groves, and stands of tall longleaf pines. When the bus passes a big magnolia, he thinks of his Tree and remembers the puffs of air. The Tree Friend. Grandmam had always said she never felt alone when she was at the Tree. Could it be that whatever it was had been Grandmam's Tree Friend? Could it be that whatever it was knew that he was her grandson? He gives his head a shake. Probably all in his imagination.

The bus driver announces the time as they pull into the filling station at Crowley. It's 11:45. The cafe where Mama works is a couple of blocks up the street. Billy's pretty sure she'll get mad when she sees him. But she's not going to see him right away. He'd heard Pap talk on the phone about Western Auto and about Catfish Cabins. Those are the places to look for Fat Man. The Western Auto is new; he doesn't know exactly where it is, but Crowley's downtown is so small, that shouldn't be a problem. He doesn't remember ever going to Catfish Cabins, but he's heard his mama talk about fishing on the river there with his dad, and with Uncle Shay. It can't be too far, he reckons.

When he gets off the bus, he walks back and forth a bit to stretch his good leg and get used to using just the one crutch. He puts it under his left arm and holds the lunch sack in his right hand. A man in a greasy coverall is putting gas in a new Ford for a dressed-up lady. It's a fine car, all black and shiny, with gold-colored upholstery on the seats. Billy sure wishes he and Pap could afford a good car. Wouldn't have to be brand new, just newer and in better shape than Big Beulah.

The restroom on the side of the station isn't locked, so he makes use of it, then goes inside the station. There's a little counter with four stools, and behind it, a stove with a big frying pan on one of the burners. A sign says hamburgers are 20 cents. A hamburger sounds good, but he'd better save the rest of his money. He's bought a round-trip ticket, so he knows he can get home, and he has two big roast beef sandwiches and a PayDay candy bar, but if he doesn't find Punchy pretty fast, he may be needing what little money he has left. Right now he's mighty thirsty and a soft drink won't cost but a nickel. He sits down at the counter.

When the man comes in from filling up the Ford and washing its windshield, he puts the gas money in the cash register. Billy plunks down a nickel and asks for a Coca Cola. The guy wipes off his hands with a greasy rag, lifts up the top of the drink tub, and fishes around in the mushy ice until he finds a Coke among the Nehi Oranges and Dr. Peppers and R.C. Colas. He hooks the cap of the bottle on the opener fastened to the side of the tub, pulls it off, and hands the cold drink to Billy. Boy howdy, does it ever taste good!

Greasy Guy sits down in a beat-up swivel chair by an old oak desk that's just about covered by a mess of papers. Papers, three dirty coffee mugs, a big full ashtray, and a newspaper partly spread out. Grease everywhere. Billy decides maybe he'd just as soon not have a hamburger made in this place by Greasy Guy. He pulls out his PayDay, making sure the man sees that it comes from his lunch sack and not the rack of candy bars sitting on the counter. As he unwraps it, he decides it's time to get some information.

"Can you tell me where the Western Auto store is, sir?"

"Up the street, middle of the fourth block. What do you need? I may have it here."

"My grandpap knows somebody that works there and I have a message for him."

"Yeah? Who's that? I probably know him; I know everybody around here."

"Mac somebody."

"That'd be Mac Albert. He works there now and again." Greasy Guy looks him over. "You came in on the bus, didn't you? Where you from?"

Billy takes a big bite of PayDay and makes a show of not being able to talk. When he gets about half of the bite down, he mumbles through the rest, "Lettston. I'm supposed to meet somebody at the cafe, but it ain't time yet."

"Who'd that be?"

Billy swallows and points outside. "Hey! You got two customers just drove up."

Greasy Guy grabs his rag and heads for the gas pumps. As soon as he gets started pumping gas, Billy gulps down the rest of his drink, sets the bottle on the counter, gets his crutch under his arm and is out the door and headed up the street.

He plans on going to the cafe first. Not to go in; he just wants to see for sure if Mama is there. He takes out an old John Deere cap of Pap's that he's stuck in a pocket, and puts it on his head, pulling it down over his hair, far enough to shade his eyes. He knows he's grown some since Mama last saw him and he's gotten thinner and he's wearing a blue plaid shirt she's never seen.

Billy stays on the opposite side of the street and steps into a little alcove that shelters the Five and Dime entrance across from the cafe. He keeps his crutch behind him, out of sight. He has a good view of the cafe but doesn't see his mother. The place is pretty full. He waits. Sure enough, after a few minutes she comes out of the kitchen with a tray and puts plates of food on a table by the window where four guys are sitting. She stands there for a few minutes. It looks like she's just shooting the breeze with them. Then she goes back into the kitchen with the tray.

Billy knows from what he heard Pap say on the phone that his mama will be at the cafe until 9:30. The next thing to do is find that Western Auto store. He starts up the street.

CHAPTER THIRTY

MR. BIKE MAN

The Western Auto store windows are full of car stuff and fishing stuff and hunting stuff. There's a red Western Flyer boy's bicycle and a blue girl's bicycle, too. Billy stands there leaning on his crutch, taking it all in. Boy, does he wish he could get that red bicycle. And one of those big hunting knives. He thinks about the knife Uncle Shay gave him and decides he's for sure gonna ask Mama about it again. He'll be 13 in two months—that's plenty old enough to have a good knife. He wonders if she still has it. Maybe it got lost when she moved. Or maybe she's sold it. Or given it to somebody. She'd better not have sold it to Fat Man.

That reminds him of what he's supposed to be doing. He walks into the store and makes his way through it slowly, looking at fishing rods and lures and stopping at the row of bicycles in the middle. A man in the back at the cash register counter waves at him.

"Hey there, young fellow. How can I help you? You like the looks of those bikes?" The man comes up the aisle to the bicycles.

"Yessir, I sure do. My old bike rusted out." Billy runs his hand over the back fender of a dark green beauty, pats the seat, takes hold of the handlebars. He likes this one even better than the red one. The price tag says $24.98.

"Isn't that a corker?" The man is smiling, enjoying watching Billy admire the bike. "And you're needing a new one. Want to take it for a spin? Well, maybe not, with that crutch and all."

"Yessir, I couldn't ride it now. Anyhow, I'll probably have to get a used one. I can't afford these. I just came in to see if somebody was here. His name is Mac. I heard he might have a hunting dog for sale."

"That'd be Mac Albert. He works here weekends sometimes, but I haven't needed him for a while. I think he's been picking up odd jobs here and there, mostly on the farms. I don't know about any dog, but could be."

"Yes sir, that's him. I'd like to ask him about that dog. You know where he lives, I reckon."

"He's staying in a cabin up by the river right now. Catfish Cabins. Used to be a fishing camp, but it wasn't doing much business and finally got sold to a fellow lives in Montgomery. He rents the cabins out to folks who need a cheap place for a while. It's about five miles up the highway. Before you and your folks drive up there, though, you bring them in to see this bike. Where are they, anyway?"

"At the cafe. I don't think my mama's gonna let me get a brand new bike, but I'll see what she says."

Billy heads for the front door, taking in all the hunting and fishing equipment along the way. There sure is a lot of it. Then he remembers his manners and stops to thank the man who, it turns out, is right behind him.

"Thank you sir, thanks a lot."

Mr. Bike Man looks like he's about to ask some more questions. So Billy hurries on out the door. Mr. Bike Man comes out, too.

"You're getting along real good on that crutch. What happened? You bust your ankle?"

"Sprained it. Fell out of a tree. I got to get on back to the cafe now. Maybe we'll be by later on."

"I'm counting on it. See y'all then. Maybe I can make you a deal."

Billy walks back in the direction of the cafe, as fast as he can with the crutch slowing him down. When he gets halfway down the block, he looks around. Mr. Bike Man has gone back into the

Western Auto, so Billy stops and looks at the display window of a shoe store until he catches his breath. There's a big clock on the corner at the bank and it shows 12:42. He's spent more time in the store than he meant to. He pulls out a sandwich and unwraps the wax paper. The roast beef's dry, even with all the mayonnaise he put on the bread. No water fountain in sight. He wishes he had another soft drink—a Nehi Orange, this time. Well, at least now the lunch bag is small enough to go into his pants pocket. His fingers are stiff from holding it.

He looks back at the clock and thinks about how long it's going to take him to go five miles on a crutch.

CHAPTER THIRTY-ONE

MR. TRACTOR MAN

Billy figures he's been going for maybe an hour and probably hasn't walked even a mile, but he's got to stop. His underarm is sore from the wooden crutch; he hadn't thought to wrap something on it for a cushion. He's tired and very thirsty. Two cars have passed him, but they were full of people and didn't stop to offer him a ride.

Most everything is farm land. No shade to walk under and with the sun beating down it feels like about 100 degrees. Even two hours up from Lettston it's still mighty hot. When he spies a clump of small oaks on the right side of the road, bordering part of a field, he takes advantage of it. He hobbles over and gets down on his knees to brush away a thick layer of dead leaves.

Getting off that crutch, stretching out under an umbrella of branches, on ground that is kind of cool where it's been buried in leaves—well, Billy feels a lot better. He can hear the roar of a tractor off a distance in the field, and the noise is soothing. He'd had little sleep the night before, what with worrying about the trip, and he's plenty tired from walking with the crutch. He'll rest fifteen or twenty minutes, then be on his way to find Fat Man.

When he wakes up, the sun is quite a ways over to the west. He's sure slept more than fifteen minutes. It must be three o'clock, at least. As he gets up off the ground, he puts weight on his left foot. Dang, that hurts. He sits back down and takes a few bites of the second dry sandwich. He sure could use some water. He thinks about a canteen he saw in the Sears Roebuck catalog one time—that's what he needs right now. He bets the Western Auto has canteens. Well, anyway, time to get going. But he knows he won't make it to the Catfish Cabins before night unless he catches a ride.

He's back on the road and has just gotten a rhythm going with the crutch when he hears that tractor coming. It's small and bright red and rolls across the field and up to the road and stops right by him. The man driving it is skinnier than Pap and older, too, Billy thinks. But he doesn't spend much time looking at the man because of what he sees fastened onto the back of the tractor. It's a small wooden seat with a short, slatted back.

"Where in tarnation are you headed for on that crutch, boy?" The old man doesn't cut the tractor motor, so he's yelling.

Billy yells back. "Up to the Catfish Cabins, sir."

"That's more than four miles. You ain't going to make it on no bum leg. You climb on that seat back there. I put it on for my great-grandboy." He jerks his thumb back over his shoulder. Billy is climbing into the seat almost before the invitation is finished.

"Be careful now, son. Keep your feet right in the middle, away from those tires. Prop 'em up on that board there. Hand me your crutch, I got a spot for it."

Billy leans up to give Mr. Tractor Man the crutch. When he sits back and props his feet, his knees come up almost to his chin. It's not real comfortable, especially with his sore ankle, but he's not going to look any gift horses in the mouth. *Or gift tractors*, he thinks.

"Thank you, sir. Thank you very much. This is a nice tractor," Billy yells.

Mr. Tractor Man turns around to yell back. "It's new. A Farmall Cub. Nothing like a Farmall. I see you got a John Deere cap. You a farmer boy? What're you doing, trying to walk all the way up there on a crutch? Who you going to see? What's your name?"

It's a lot of questions and Billy doesn't want to answer any of them. He mumbles that he hadn't known it was so far.

"What's that? You got to speak up, boy. What did you say your name was?"

"It's Will," yells Billy. That's true. William Alvan Burnette, Jr. is his full name. Will sounds older than Billy. He runs his finger over the WAB on his daddy's leather wristband.

"Bet you're thirsty, ain't you, Will?" Mr. Tractor Man leans backward to hand Billy a big jar with some water in it. "You finish that off. Ain't much left, but something's better'n nothing."

Billy unscrews the lid and drains the jar. It tastes even better than Coca Cola to his parched mouth. "Thank you, sir," he yells. He wedges the jar between his chest and knees, rests his chin on it, and pretends he's gone to sleep. It works pretty well. Every now and then Mr. Tractor Man looks back and yells something and Billy gives a start, like he's almost waking up, mumbles something, and puts his head down again.

The tractor doesn't go very fast. Traffic picks up in both directions and they often have to pull over to let folks go by, so it takes a while to go the rest of the way to the cabins. When they get there Mr. Tractor Man pulls the Farmall across the road to the entrance, stops and lets the tractor idle. Billy climbs out of the seat, a little deaf from the tractor's noise and still vibrating inside from its motion. He hands over the water jar and the old man gives him the crutch. Billy gets it under his arm and feels steadier.

"Thank you, sir," he yells.

Mr. Tractor Man pulls out his pocket watch and yells that it's going on four o'clock and he has to get home. Billy is surprised to see him turn and head back down the way they came. It looks like he's gone out of his way to get Billy to the cabins.

"I'm much obliged, sir," yells Billy, as loud as he can. Then he turns and looks at the narrow dirt road that runs between two rows of cabins.

"Well," he says, "I'm here."

CHAPTER THIRTY-TWO

CATFISH CABINS

A faded sign that says CATFISH CABINS is on a pole over at the left side of the entrance. It has a picture of a pale, whiskered fish jumping up in the water. Billy is glad to see a telephone booth right by the pole. He's going to need to call his mom at some point; he sure can't make it back down to Crowley on his own. The booth door is open and he takes a quick look. The phone's hanging there, a little crooked, with a dog-eared telephone book on the shelf under it. It's a pay phone. He jingles the change in his pocket to reassure himself.

A whole bunch of rusty mailboxes on posts are lined up just past the booth. Farther on down the dirt road, two rows of weather beaten cabins face each other. To the sides and back, big trees and bushes and ivy look like they're trying to take over the whole place.

Six kids stand between the first two cabins in the road, watching Billy. Two of them are boys, bigger than Billy. Thoughts of the Randalls run through his mind. He pushes his armpit up off the crutch and draws himself up tall as he can. The other four kids are girls, one about his size and three smaller. They're all carrying books; it looks like maybe they got off a school bus not long before Billy got off the tractor. He walks up to them.

"Hey," he says in as deep and loud a voice as he can muster. "Anybody seen a little brown dog? I'm up here visiting, and he's disappeared. Somebody told me they thought they'd seen him on a pickup belonging to a guy that lives here."

Heads shake. They're all still staring at him.

"We saw you get off that tractor," one of the boys says.

"How's come you're on a crutch?" asks the other. "You a cripple?"

Billy thinks of the Randalls again. They love to call Rick a cripple. "Naw, I ain't no cripple. Sprained my ankle. So the fellow on the tractor gave me a ride. My mom's going to pick me up later. You know which is Mac Albert's cabin? He's the one might of seen my dog."

"It's in the back. I'll show you," the bigger girl says. Close up, she's a little taller than Billy. She has brown eyes and real curly black hair pulled back in a short ponytail.

The boys laugh and one of them says in a high voice, "I can show you." He bats his eyes and acts like he's flouncing a skirt. Everybody laughs, including Billy.

It doesn't seem to bother Miss Ponytail. "Oh hey, Jake, you make a great girl. I'll have to lend you one of my skirts so you can do it right. I've got a pretty pink one that's just about your size."

The other boy laughs even harder. He hits his friend on the shoulder. "Whooee, Jake, can't wait to see that. We'll have to call you Jackie. Or maybe Jack-wuh-leen!"

Miss Ponytail turns to Billy. "Come on, Mr. Albert's cabin is in the back. I haven't seen a dog with him, but I haven't even seen *him* lately. He's gone a lot. Doesn't have much to do with anybody here." She motions him to follow her. The rest of the kids trail along.

"What's your name?" asks one of the boys.

"It's Bill." Oh shoot, he shoulda said Will.

"Bill what?" asks the other one.

"Bill Burnette."

"There's a Miz Burnette that works at the cafe in Crowley," says Miss Ponytail.

"Yeah, that's my mama."

"We call her Miss Allie. She's nice. Real pretty, too." She looks at Billy closely. "But I haven't seen you around here before."

"No, I live with my grandpap down at Lettston right now. Mama's just working up here for a while. She grew up here. She's going to move back with us soon as she figures out what to do with her house." That maybe isn't so true but it sounds better than saying his mother doesn't want to live with him.

They're at the end of the dirt road and Miss Ponytail marches right up on the little porch of number 20, last cabin on the right, and knocks on the door. Billy's stomach knots up. He hadn't meant for her to do that. He's not ready yet. What'll he'll say if Fat Man comes to the door? He doesn't want to say anything in front of all these kids. What'll Fat Man do when he sees him: the "Squirrel." Billy's stomach unknots when there's no answer to the knock.

"I didn't figure he was here, because his old pickup's gone," says Miss Ponytail. "No telling when he'll be back. He doesn't have a regular job. Are you going to wait? When's your mama coming for you?"

"When she gets off work. Y'all can go on now. I'll wait around 'til he comes back."

The kids aren't in any hurry to leave, but about that time, somebody yells from a cabin up front for Jake and somebody else calls for Elsie. It's getting close to supper time. Pretty soon they've all gone except for Miss Ponytail.

"You better go on, too," says Billy. He needs to get rid of her before Fat Man comes. "Your folks'll be worried."

"I don't have to go yet. Daddy won't be home until 5:30, maybe later. He works at the lumber mill up the road. I'll have to warm up some supper for him in a little bit."

"What about your mama?"

"She's gone."

Billy thought about his own mama and doesn't ask where hers has gone. Anyway, Miss Ponytail doesn't give him time.

"What are you going to do if Mr. Albert doesn't have your dog?" she asks. "You could put up some signs. You could put a 'Lost and Found' ad in the paper."

Cabin 19, across from Fat Man's place, isn't rented out, so they sit on the steps there and talk. Billy finds he's glad for the company. Keeps him from worrying so much about what he's going to do when Fat Man shows up.

Her name is Annette and she's fourteen and in the eighth grade and she's only lived in Crowley five months. She says her daddy has just been made foreman at the lumber mill and is making more money, so now they're going to look for a real house. Her daddy wants something with a little land, so they can have a garden. They moved to Crowley from Louisiana. There's a Crowley there, too, but they didn't live there, they lived in Lafayette. Billy is glad she likes to talk and doesn't ask him many questions. When it begins to get dark, she stands up.

"We're in number 16, two rows up, Bill. Stop by there before you leave. If you get your dog back I'd like to meet him." She stands there thinking for a moment. "Oh yeah. You saw the telephone booth up at the front. We don't have phones in the cabins, so if you need to call Miss Allie, you'll have to use it. It takes a nickel."

When she leaves, Billy walks all the way around Cabin 20. The wood door on the back is closed but the screen door is sagging open. There's one window in the back, kind of high up. There's a window in the middle of each side of the cabin. All the windows have screens. Two bigger windows on each side of the front door are raised a few inches and held up by sticks. No curtains, just shades rolled up to the top, so he can look into all but the high-up back window and see just about everything. Nothing in the bedroom but a bed and a big chest of drawers and piles of clothes on the floor. One of the drawers is pulled halfway out and the handle's hanging off.

He goes to the front and looks through the window to the right of the door. There's a small living room area. A big chair against the front wall faces the back of the cabin and takes up most of the space. A little round table is to one side of it, and on the other side a radio sits on an upended wooden crate. A smaller chair is over near the wall, slanted to face the big one. Beyond, there's a small wood dining table and two straight-backed wood chairs. A tiny kitchen area is at the back of the cabin. Billy sees the door to the bedroom on the left wall of the living room space and another door on that wall, right across from the kitchen. Billy figures that second one has to be the bathroom.

He checks out the cabin next to Fat Man's, number 18. No sign of anybody there. He walks over to the cabin across from it. There's a car parked on the left side. Lights are on and he hears a radio, but the shades are pulled down at all the windows and he can't see in. Annette has told him it's an old couple that are just there for a few weeks while their house is getting fixed from storm damage. She said they were real nice, but didn't hear well and mostly stayed in, except for Sundays, when they went to church.

After he's seen everything, Billy goes back to the cabin across from Fat Man's place, and gets behind a big oak tree that's near the back. He's hidden, but he can see the door of Cabin 20 when he peeks around.

He has a friend. Miss Pony Tail. Annette. And there's a telephone and he has a nickel for it. But his stomach is beginning to churn again. He leans back against the tree and traces the initials on his wristband over and over while he waits.

CHAPTER THIRTY-THREE

PUNCHY

By the time Billy hears the sound of the old pickup turning into Catfish Cabins' dirt road, it has gotten darker. He lays down on the ground and looks around the oak tree. Fat Man drives past his cabin, pulls in at the side, and sits there for a moment with the motor still running. Billy sees a movement in the back of the truck. Punchy! The little dog barks and tries to jump over the side of the truck, but he's tied to something. Billy has to keep himself from jumping up and running to grab him.

Punchy keeps barking and lunging, trying to get free of his tether. His nose and ears point toward Billy. Before Fat Man shuts the motor off, the little dog's sharp ears hear the voice he's been listening for ever since he was stolen away.

Billy says just two words, "Quiet, Punchy." He says them low. He thinks Punchy's ears can hear him and that Fat Man's cannot, not over that noisy engine. Punchy doesn't make another sound, but he stays where he is, looking over the pickup's side.

Fat Man slides over and gets out on the passenger side—the driver's door is roped shut. The big man limps around to the other side, reaches over into the back of the truck and unties Punchy from the tool box but keeps hold of the rope tied to the little dog. "Okay, you worthless mutt. Get on down from there." He yanks Punchy over the side. The little dog falls to the ground, but springs up immediately, still looking toward where Billy is hidden.

"Come on here. Some hunter you turned out to be. You ain't worth a plug nickel. Sport's welcome to you." Fat Man reaches into the truck cab, brings out a rifle, and tucks it under his arm. He pulls the little dog around to the front of the cabin, opens the screen door, unlocks the wood door, and turns on the overhead light. He jerks Punchy into the cabin. Punchy isn't making a sound but he's resisting the rope with all his might. Billy watches. He's so mad he forgets about his nervous stomach.

Fat Man props the rifle in a corner. Still holding Punchy's rope, he opens the windows wide, unlocks and opens the back door and pulls on the screen, forcing it into the door frame and latching it. He turns on the light in the kitchen. He leaves the front wood door open, closing that screen, too, but not fastening it. Billy crawls to the front of Cabin 19 and gets behind a row of big azalea bushes. On his tiptoes—*ouch*, that hurts his ankle—he can see a lot through Cabin 20's open door and windows. He watches Fat Man tie Punchy's rope to one of the dining table legs, get himself a beer out of the refrigerator, and switch on a big fan that's sitting on the table. Then he plops himself down in the big chair, and turns the radio on.

Billy leaves his crutch under the azaleas. He takes his shoes off and, carrying them, limps across the road. He crouches down to go under the side window of Fat Man's cabin, gets to the back and sits on the ground. He tries to stop shaking. He's still mad, but he's plenty scared, too.

When he settles down some, he moves back to where he can see in the side window, almost straight to where Punchy is tied to the table leg. Punchy has been drinking water from a bowl under the table, but when he catches Billy's scent, he swivels his head toward the window. Fat Man swigs down his beer, gets up and limps to the kitchen, and disappears through the door opposite the sink. *Yep*, Billy thinks, *that's got to be the bathroom.*

Billy is at the front door in about half a second. He opens the screen door and tiptoes in, not even noticing how his left ankle is doing. The radio's turned up high and the fan is loud. Billy kneels down and Punchy jumps into his arms and licks his face. "Quiet, Punchy," he whispers. The little dog gets still. Billy had thought he could just slip the rope off the table leg, but the leg has knobby rings that stick out and keep the rope from sliding, so that won't work. He looks at the knot there and the one at Punchy's neck. The one on the little dog seems looser, so he goes to work on it. It's a hard knot. He hasn't made any headway when he hears the toilet flush in the bathroom. "Quiet, Punchy. I'll be back," he whispers, and scoots out the door to squat down on the ground under the side window.

When Fat Man comes out of the bathroom, the screen door isn't quite closed. He goes over and pulls it to. Looks at it, then at Punchy. "I thought I heard you scrabbling around out here. Something come up to the door? Well, you didn't bark, did you? Just laid there and done nothing. Big watch dog, too, ain't you? Worthless piece of dog flesh. Sport'll be over here after while. I'm gonna tell him he can have you."

He opens the refrigerator and gets out another beer and a bowl. "Got some chicken here. Not that you deserve any." He holds a piece over toward Punchy. The dog doesn't even look at it. His eyes are glued to the window. "Not good enough for you? Suit yourself. Maybe Sport's mama'll cook you up something real special tomorrow." Fat Man guffaws at that, then turns the radio down and sprawls in the chair with his beer and cold chicken.

Billy hopes Fat Man will be like Pap is after he drinks, and go to sleep in his chair, but the big guy shows no signs of that. After the news ends, he turns the dial to a country music station. Billy gets more and more worried. If Sport is coming over, there'll be two of them to deal with. They might even be going back to the Tree tonight. He needs help. Cabin 16, two rows up, Annette had said. He puts his shoes on.

The wood door to 16 is closed but the windows are open and lights are on. There's no car or truck, so he reckons her daddy hasn't come home yet. He knocks softly and hears footsteps. Annette pulls aside the curtain over the window to the right of the door. She smiles when she sees him, unlocks the door and opens it.

"Hey, Bill. Come on in. Daddy must be having to work late but I've got stew warming. You hungry? Sit here in front of this fan and cool off. I guess Mr. Albert didn't have your dog? I heard his pickup come in. That old thing sounds like it's about ready to fall apart. You need a nickel to call Miss Allie?

"Annette, what I need is some help." Billy sounds as desperate as he feels. "I didn't tell you the whole truth. Mac Albert didn't find my dog, he stole him. He *has* got Punchy back there and I heard him say the other guy that helped him steal him is coming over and I got to get Punchy out of there before he shows up."

"Good grief, Bill! He *stole* him? That's awful! I'll sure help if I can."

"Do you have a sharp knife?"

Annette's brown eyes get bigger. "You aren't going to hurt Mr. Albert, are you? I'm not helping you do anything like that."

"No, no, it's that Punchy's tied up and I was in there once when Mr. Albert was in the bathroom and I couldn't get the rope untied and I need a knife to cut him loose. Then we have to have some place to hide until I can get my mama up here."

"You better tell me what this is all about," says Annette.

So he does. And when he's told her everything, they come up with a plan.

CHAPTER THIRTY-FOUR

PAP AND RICK

"What in the world was that boy thinking?" Pap is looking at the note that Rick has "found" under Billy's pillow. "That's just plumb crazy. Him with a bad ankle, going up there to find somebody that he don't even know where he lives and is a bad character to boot. I gotta call his mama right now. He dang sure better be with her."

He pushes himself up from the kitchen chair, stretches his back and eases himself down in the chair under the phone. When he picks up the receiver, he hears the preacher's wife talking.

"Miz Havard," he says, "excuse me, please ma'am, but I've got to make a call right now. It can't wait. Could you let me have the line for about five minutes?" Miz Havard obliges. He's glad it's her; he knows she won't listen in. Some of the others on the party line are nosy. He dials Allie's number. Her phone rings eight times before he realizes she'll still be at work. He hangs the receiver back on its hook.

"I got to have the Crowley phone book, Rick. I'm so bumfuzzled I can't remember the number of the cafe. Look in the drawer of the corner cupboard, it ought to be in there." When Rick hands him the thin book Pap's hands are shaking and it takes him a little time to find the listing. "Here it is, Crowley Cafe." He dials the four digits. There are ten rings. Finally, somebody answers.

"I need to speak to Allie Burnette," Pap says.

"She ain't allowed to take calls here." It's a surly male voice. Pap guesses it must be the new owner. Allie has told him the man isn't much fun to work for.

"This is important, sir. She's my daughter-in-law and it's about her son. Can you tell me if he's there?"

"No, he ain't. She can call you back after this crowd's gone." The man hangs up.

Pap is furious, but forces himself to calm down before dialing the number again. After it rings fifteen times, he hangs up and dials again. And again. He throws up his hands in frustration.

"He ain't gonna answer. But he said Billy Boy ain't there. And said she can call me after the crowd leaves." He gets up from the straight chair slowly, favoring his back, and goes into the living room. He looks at the corner cupboard. It would sure calm his nerves right now to have a little snort. But Rick's there and besides, he'd better be thinking clearly. "What are we going to do, Rick?" he asks.

Rick's as worried as Pap is but he doesn't want to show it. "He's all right, Mr. Burnette," he says. "He's probably waiting somewhere 'til his mama gets off from work. He wouldn't do anything silly. He's just waiting and resting up."

"Well, why wouldn't he be doing that at the cafe?"

"That man might not let him wait there. But, you know what? Crowley's got a picture show. I'll bet you that's where he is. It'd be cool in there. His mama probably gave him some money for it."

Pap wants to believe that, so he doesn't let himself think about what time picture shows open. He looks at the clock. It's 5:30. "Maybe you're right. But why wouldn't she have called to tell me he was all right?

"That man probably wouldn't let her," Rick says.

"Well," says Pap, "rush time'll be over at the cafe by 6:30 and that gosh darned fool had better answer the phone then. If he don't, I'm calling the sheriff up there."

CHAPTER THIRTY-FIVE

MISS PONY TAIL

Billy's heart is beating like it's going to come out of his chest. He is behind the big oak at Cabin 19. It's really dark. It seems like at least half an hour since he left Annette's. Fat Man's front door is still open and he's in his chair eating a candy bar. Punchy is lying still, watching the door.

Waiting for Annette is the hardest thing Billy's had to do so far. But finally, here she comes. Soon as he sees her, he runs, crouched over, to the left side of Fat Man's cabin and hides behind the pickup. He doesn't even think about his ankle. Annette walks down the dirt road and marches right up to Fat Man's door.

"Mr. Albert, you've got a call," she announces in a loud voice. "I was down at the mailboxes and heard the phone ring. I told him I'd come get you."

Mac gets up from his chair, looking disgusted, and comes to the door. "He say who he was?"

"No sir, he didn't." She turns and goes back up the road to her cabin.

Mac had taken off his boots and now he has to put them on again. "Probably the idiot calling to say he can't get a ride over here," he grumbles. He looks at Punchy as he goes by. "Stupid dog," he says. He goes out, closing the door behind him, and limps up the road to the telephone booth.

Billy is right up against the cabin. He stays low, and sticks his head around. When Fat Man gets to the fourth row of cabins, Billy scoots around to the front door, opening it just enough to slide in and shutting it, very quietly, behind him. He touches his finger to his lips. "Quiet, Punchy," he says. "I'm gonna get you out of here." He has a big, sharp, butcher knife in his hand. It takes him about three minutes to saw through the rope, just before where it's tied to Punchy's neck. He grabs his dog, gets out the door, and shuts it tight. No Fat Man in sight now.

He slips past the back of the next cabin and runs to Annette's. She's waiting, with the kitchen door open. As soon as he and Punchy are in, she closes and locks it. Billy doesn't slow down. He's breathing hard and sweating bad when he and Punchy plop down on the floor of the little bathroom. He reaches up and locks the door. It's plenty hot in the crowded space. "We gotta stay real still, Punch." Punchy curls up in his lap quietly, licking Billy's hand. Billy strokes his little dog's head and back and can't get enough of hugging him, even hot as it is. Punchy seems okay, maybe dirtier than usual.

Annette turns the radio up loud, points the fan toward the stove, and gets busy with the stew pot. It isn't long before there's a knock on the door. She takes her time going. She's carrying the big wooden spoon that she's been stirring with, and holds it with both hands to keep them from shaking. She moves the curtain to look out the window, then unlocks and opens the door.

"There wasn't nobody on the phone," Mac says.

"There wasn't?" Annette looks surprised. "He must've hung up. Or...you know how that phone is; sometimes it just quits working." She sounds concerned. "And you had to walk all the way up there on your bad leg for nothing."

"Did he sound like a young fellow?"

"I don't know. There was static on the line. I'm sorry I didn't get his name."

"Well, it's not your fault. I got somebody supposed to come by and I was thinking it might be him. Maybe I oughta call him. I'll have to get a nickel." Mac doesn't turn to go, though.

Annette takes the hint. "I can lend you a nickel, Mr. Albert. Save you some steps on that leg. Hold on."

Mac stands at the door while she goes to the kitchen, opens a drawer, moves things around in it. She opens another one, looks through it. "We always try to keep some for the phone but I don't see...oh, wait a minute, there may be one up here." She reaches up and gets a jar off a shelf over the sink. "We save pennies and sometimes there's a nickel or dime mixed in. Yeah, here's a couple of nickels."

She goes back to the door, taking her time, straightening up papers and books on the dining table, keeping her hands busy because they're still trembling.

"Sorry this place is such a mess. I was doing my homework and the time got away from me. Daddy likes me to have supper ready when he gets home." She waves the spoon at the clock on the wall. "He'll be here any minute." She hands a nickel to Mac.

"Thanks. I'll get it back to you tonight." Mac says gruffly as he turns to go.

"No rush. Tomorrow's fine," says Annette. "You probably oughta stay off that leg as much as you can."

When the big man leaves, Annette locks the door and stands there hugging herself tight to stop quivering. Thinking, *how long will it be before he gets back home and discovers Punchy's gone?* She turns the radio volume up and whispers through the bathroom door for Billy to stay there and stay quiet. Then she goes back to the stove and stirs the stew some more. She's thinking, not paying attention, and it slops over the sides of the pan. When she finally hears a loud knock at the door, she jumps and drops the spoon on the floor. She waits, and the knock is repeated, louder.

"Just a minute," she yells. "I got something boiling over."

She wets a dishrag to wipe off the stove. Then she picks up the spoon and cleans the floor where it dropped. She's got stew on her face and dress when she makes her way slowly to the door, holding the dishrag. "Who is it?" she calls.

"You know who it is. It's Mac Albert. I want to talk to you, young lady."

Annette unlocks the door and opens it a crack. "Sorry, Mr. Albert, I've got stew all over the place in here." Her voice sounds too high to her, and her hands are shaking so much that she's wiping them with the messy dishrag.

Mac's face is beet red. "Somebody's took my dog. You got anything to say about that, missy? It's mighty strange, it happenin' when you sent me off to take a call from somebody that wasn't there. I'm gonna have me a look around here." Annette tries to shut the door. Mac shoves it open, pushes her aside, and charges in. He looks around, goes into the bedroom, comes out and heads for the bathroom.

Just then, a pickup pulls up outside.

CHAPTER THIRTY-SIX

MAMA

When Billy limps into the Crowley Cafe on his crutch, holding Punchy against his chest with his right arm, Allie Burnette is refilling ice tea glasses at a long table decorated with balloons. She stops. Her eyes get big. She sets the pitcher down on the table and goes to her son. She looks at the crutch, at his foot, at the rest of him. His hair is dirty. His eyes are red. He has grass in his hair. His clothes are a mess. Punchy doesn't look any better. And they both smell. She puts her arms around them.

"My lord!" she says.

Before Billy can say a word, a big red-headed man in a dirty apron comes out from behind the counter. "Get that mutt outta here. And you get back to work, Allie."

"You wait a minute, Doug, this is my son. What in the world, Billy Boy? What are you doing up here?"

"I came to get Punchy."

Doug sees that customers are watching. He moves closer and his voice gets lower but meaner. "You the one that old man was calling about? I told him your mama was busy. She's still busy. Outside with the dog, kid. Dogs ain't allowed." The big man looks at Allie and nods toward the birthday table. "You get those folks taken care of."

Allie erupts. "Pap called and you didn't *tell* me? You didn't tell me he called about my *son*?"

Everybody in the cafe is watching. Doug lowers his voice more. "You get them out of here and get back to work if you want this job."

Allie's voice gets a lot louder. "You know what? I don't think I *do* want this job." She moves away from Billy and Punchy, takes off her apron, and throws it on the floor.

Now her boss yells. "You're fired!"

Allie yells back. "I quit!" She grabs her purse from behind the counter, puts her arm around Billy's back, and leads him out of the cafe. He's still hugging Punchy to his chest.

Annette and her daddy are right out front, sitting in their truck. They've been watching the action in the cafe. Mr. Powers leans out the window. "Everything okay? You need a ride somewhere?"

"Mama, this is Mr. Powers and Annette," says Billy. "They helped me get Punchy back."

"I've seen y'all in the cafe," says Allie. "I sure thank you, Mr. Powers. You too, Annette. But you'll have to excuse us. This young man's got a whole lot of explaining to do. Oh, and I appreciate your offer of a ride, but I've got my car."

Mr. Powers puts his hand out to shake Mama's hand. "Glad to be of service, ma'am. We need to get on back home, but you let me know if there's anything else I can do. You've got a fine boy there."

As the truck drives away, Annette puts her head out the window and yells, "Bye, Bill! Bye, Punchy!"

Allie gets Billy and Punchy into her car and they sit there while Billy tells her about his day in Crowley. He makes it short. He doesn't tell her that he knows she's the one who sent Fat Man and Pimples to kill his Tree. When he finishes, she starts up the car.

"I'm taking you home to Pap right now. We'll have to stop by the house. I need to call him, tell him you're okay. You can use the bathroom and we'll get something for you and Punchy to eat and a pillow for you. I want you to sleep all the way, you're worn out. I'll drop you off but I'm not staying. I'm coming right on back up here."

"We could wait 'til tomorrow, Mama. That's four hours driving. You prob'ly won't get back here 'til after midnight." Billy's so tired he can hardly get the words out.

"No, we're not waiting. I need to get you down there and get me back here tonight. There's things I've got to do. I've made up my mind about something."

CHAPTER THIRTY-SEVEN

BACK HOME

Billy wakes up very early Thursday morning. He tests his ankle and decides he doesn't need the crutch. After he's dressed he goes to the kitchen and sees Pap sitting out on the back porch with his feet propped on the rail and his eyes closed. Billy doesn't want to disturb him, so he lets Punchy out the front door. He wants to check on something there, anyway, before Rick comes.

The Weatherlings are on the front porch. Gulf Breeze is sitting on the railing; Autumn and Summer are rocking in the chairs. Autumn stops when she hears the screen door open, Summer doesn't. Billy sees what he's looking for: the movement of a rocker. Punchy makes a beeline for the other rocker, the one that's still. He stands up with his paws on the seat and whines. Billy holds his hand up in the air. It's not a breeze that's causing the other chair to move. "Come here, Punch," he says. He stands there, waiting, and, sure enough, just as Punchy comes to him, Billy feels three puffs of cool air on his neck.

The Tree Friend is here, he thinks. *The Friend that puffs cool air and rocks in chairs and was at the Tree the night of the fight. Could that be who…what…caused the crazy storm that drove Fat Man and Pimples away?* He thinks it could be. "Thank you," he whispers to the air.

Autumn beams, and blows another puff. Billy smiles. He goes back inside to finish getting ready for school. He's not surprised when Punchy stays on the porch.

Later on, Billy is disappointed when his little dog doesn't come with him and Rick to the bus stop. Maybe Punchy's over being dognapped and is just happy to be back home. But Billy suspects the Tree Friend may have something to do with it.

Rick had shown up in time to have breakfast with Billy and Pap and hear the story. It was mostly news to Pap, too, since Billy had gone right to bed when his mama brought him home the night before, and Allie didn't have time to tell Pap much. Now the boys are walking down the road to Rick's house to catch the school bus and still talking about what all had happened. Billy's still using one crutch, but only because Pap insisted.

"Boy howdy, Billy Burnette, if you ain't something! What a time you had! Oh man! I wish I coulda been with you!" Rick slaps his friend on the back. "I'm sorry I couldn't wait with your grandpap 'til you got home last night, but I asked him if I could come back this morning as soon as I ate breakfast, and I was so glad he took the hint and said come and eat with y'all."

"I needed you bad in Crowley, Rick," says Billy. "But that girl, Annette, she was great! And her daddy...when he pulled up in his pickup just in time to run Fat Man off! Telling Fat Man he'd have the law on him for barging into the cabin and scaring Annette, and for stealing my dog. When we got in Mr. Power's truck and drove down the cabin road to get your crutch, you should've seen old Fat Man! Tried to run after us but he's too fat and you could tell his knee was hurting him. And when we came back by him to get on the highway, all he could do was yell and shake his fists at us. Folks were sticking their heads out of the cabins to see what was going on."

Rick was laughing hard, even though he had just heard the whole thing at breakfast. Then he thought of something and turned serious. "So your mama went on back to Crowley after she brought you and Punchy home. If she quit her job, what's her hurry? Why didn't she spend the night with you?"

"Pap wanted her to stay. He didn't want her to drive back up there so late, by herself, but she didn't pay any attention to him. Said she had to get back and pack up and see about renting out the house. She's gonna live with us again."

"Why don't she just sell that house?"

"She grew up in it. That's one reason she decided to go back there and work when she couldn't find any job she wanted around here. She loves that house. Uncle Shay wants to sell it, but she says no, not their family place. After Grandma and Grandpa Cramer died, it was just sitting there empty 'til she moved in."

"Billy, you shoulda seen your grandpap's face when she called him and told him you was with her. He'd about worried himself to death. He was pretty near ready to call the sheriff in Crowley."

"Yeah, he was happy to see us. And Punchy was so glad to be home, he was running around in circles. I was just as glad as he was, but too tired to run around. And my ankle was hurting some. It was mighty good to get into that bed. But I'm glad Pap said I could go to school today—I've got a lot of catching up to do."

Rick grinned. "It won't take you long." Then another thought struck him. "Bill, yesterday I got to thinking about that chain saw. I hope you don't mind me going into Lost Lane without you, but I went and dragged it up to this end of the lane. It's still in the sack and still dry. I covered it with leaves, but you won't have any trouble finding it."

"Thanks, Rick. You can go to Lost Lane any time you want to, buddy. Just don't let anybody see you." *That durned chain saw,* he thought to himself. *What if Fat Man and Pimples come back for it?*

CHAPTER THIRTY-EIGHT

HERO

The kids gather round as soon as Billy and Rick show up in front of the Showers' house. Word has gotten around about Billy's trip to Crowley to save Punchy. They want all the details. When the bus comes they're still all excited and asking questions. Mr. Davis says, "Y'all settle down, now," but he grins at Billy. Al and Sam sit across from Billy and Rick and the twins take their usual seat behind the hero and his friend. Al and Sam have a lot more to ask Billy and the little girls lean forward, taking it all in.

The bus is almost to school before Billy and Rick realize that the Randalls have moved May and Fay to the back and have taken their place.

"Hey there, Silly Boy! You been up to Crowley beatin' up on some old man? We missed you, didn't we, Roy?" Billy waits for the big hands to close around his neck. They don't.

Roy chimes in. "Sure did. So that mutt of yours must be some kinda famous huntin' dog, gettin' stole like that and all."

"You sayin' you broke in the guy's house and took Punchy right out from under this old man's nose?" Matt sounds skeptical.

Roy doesn't, though. "What's this about you havin' a knife? Did you have to cut him? How old was he? How big was he? Did he hurt you any?"

Billy looks at them, then turns back around, but Rick pipes up, "He's a huge guy but Bill was too smart for him, that's all. He played a trick to get him out of the cabin and then cut Punchy loose with the knife and took him to another cabin and hid and then got somebody to take him and Punchy out of there. You know, Bill went all the way to Crowley with a sprained ankle and then he went five more miles to where that old dog thief lives."

"Is that so?" Matt looks at Billy. "We want to hear it from you."

"That's pretty much what happened. I had some help getting Punchy. And I caught a ride once I got up there. And I had a ride back to here. But that's pretty much it."

"Well, how about that, Roy, we sure enough got us a tough guy and a famous huntin' dog, to boot." Matt laughs and he slaps Billy on the shoulder. "So when you and your dog gonna take us huntin'?"

Billy looks like he's thinking about it. "We may just do that, Matt. Maybe when my ankle gets better you and Roy can go out with me and Punch and my grandpap. And Rick." He puts his arm around Rick's shoulder. "Rick here knows all the best places." Rick gives Billy a look.

Matt looks at Rick. "That so? Well, it's a deal, buddy," says Matt. And he slaps Billy on the shoulder again.

The four boys get off the bus together, but Matt and Roy spot one of the seniors on the other side of the street in a convertible, and they head over to look at it. Billy and Rick walk along with the other kids, who still want to talk about the big adventure. As they make their way to the door, Rick says in a low voice, "Billy, you know I don't know anything about places to hunt."

"You will," says Billy, with a great big grin. "Just as soon as Pap and I tell you."

CHAPTER THIRTY-NINE

CARVED ON THE TREE

"Stay here with Pap, Punchy," says Autumn.

Autumn is going back to her Tree. She needs to do some thinking. Summer and Gulf Breeze are at the Underpier. She's no longer afraid they will disappear. Gulf Breeze likes her now, and Summer tolerates her. In fact, Summer has been taking her here and there on the beach, telling her about gulls and terns and pelicans, and creatures like jellyfish and starfish that have washed up onto the sand, and all sorts of things. Summer loves to show off what she knows. That's all right with Autumn. She needs to learn all she can. Of course, she suspects that Summer is mostly spending time with her to avoid listening to Gulf Breeze, who keeps trying to convince her that her continued hot presence is not good for the Deep South Greenstuff.

Autumn spends the rest of Thursday morning in her leaf cocoon at the top of the Tree, thinking about all that's happened since East Wind dropped her off a week ago. Sol hasn't quite reached the top of the sky when Autumn hears sounds from the bushes that hide Lost Lane. She glides over and looks down to see Pap squeezing through, dragging a little step stool. Punchy is right behind him. Autumn quickly moves to a tall tree a distance away and downwind, so Punchy's nose won't find her.

Pap circles the Tree, feeling it with his hand, touching the gash. Punchy sniffs around on the ground. Autumn is afraid Pap is checking to see how much more it'll take to kill the tree. She watches him use the step stool to get onto the walk-up limb, right near the tree trunk, and then he starts to climb. *He's too old to do that,* she thinks. But he only climbs a little way before he eases around toward the back of the trunk. *That's where the heart is. SJB loves AJB,* she remembers.

When he comes back down, he stops on the climb-up branch. "Sarah Jane Brown loves Alvan John Burnette." He says it out loud. "Sarah Jane. My Sally." He rubs his eyes with his hand. Punchy goes to him as he steps onto the stool and eases himself to the ground. He looks back up into the tree. "I'm sorry for what I did, Sally. Don't worry, your tree is safe." He and Punchy go back through the bushes, Pap pulling the step stool after them.

Autumn can't wait to tell Summer and Gulf Breeze what she's just heard.

CHAPTER FORTY

SURPRISE VISITOR

On Saturday morning, Pap and Billy and Punchy are having a fine breakfast of pancakes and maple syrup and sausages. Friday had been like a regular, normal, day and Billy is enjoying not being worried about anything, but Punchy starts barking and runs to the front door and, in a minute, Billy and Pap hear the sound of a motor in the driveway. They look at each other, thinking the same thing: Fat Man and Pimples.

"Sit still, Billy Boy," says Pap. He joins Punchy at the door. Billy isn't about to miss out; he's right behind Pap.

It's not Fat Man and Pimples. It's a guy in a dirty, brown, late-model Chevy. He's sitting there in the driver's seat, with his arms on top of the steering wheel and his head resting on them.

"Who is it, Pap?"

"I don't know, boy, but that car sure needs a good wash."

Billy opens the screen. He lets out a whoop when the man lifts his head. "It's Uncle Shay, Pap! It's Uncle Shay!"

Shay opens the car door and Billy is out in a flash, grabbing his uncle's hand as soon as he steps from the car. Punchy is right there, too. He catches Billy's excitement and starts in dashing around and barking.

"Hush up, Punchy. You'll run him off," Pap says as he comes down the steps and reaches for Shay's other hand to shake it. "Come on in, you're just in time for breakfast. Boy, you're a sight for sore eyes."

"You too, Pap," says Shay. "Both of you. All three of you." He hugs Billy and reaches down to pat Punchy. "I've been driving two days. I could sure use a cup of good, strong coffee."

"Coffee's made. And pancakes to go with it. How's that sound?" Pap is beaming.

"Sounds mighty good, Pap." Shay looks at Billy. "You must've grown a foot since I saw you, Billy Boy. You're gonna be tall as your daddy. I hear you've been on a pretty good trip yourself. And on a bum foot. You had any time to go to school this week?"

Billy ducks his head, but he's feeling pretty proud. "I just missed two days. I was there Monday and Thursday and yesterday. I've caught up on nearly everything."

They talk about school and Shay's trip and his new car and the weather until Shay has his fill of pancakes. Then he pours his third mug of coffee and leans back in his chair. "Mighty good, Pap. Thank you." He reaches down to scratch Punchy's neck. "Y'all been going through a bit of a hassle up here."

"Allie called you, didn't she?" says Pap.

"Yes sir, Thursday morning, early. She was fit to be tied. I told her she should have called me before all this got started. But Allie's prideful. Stubborn as a mule. Didn't want to admit she was wrong to move to Crowley, but said Billy Boy needs her now and she's moving back in with y'all."

"She tell you what I was thinking about doing? And how bad it turned out?"

"She did. I told her it was a crazy idea to begin with. Sorry Pap, but it was, even though I know you meant well. And then for her to get Mac Albert involved. He was bad news back in high school. Still is, appears like."

Pap looks over at Billy. He doesn't realize how much his grandson already knows about Allie's involvement in the plot, and he's thinking he should have sent Billy outside before this conversation got started. It's too late; the boy's drinking it all in.

Poor kid. Maybe it's just as well, though—get everything out in the open, try to get things fixed, make it up to him some way, hope he'll forgive both of them.

"I told her I was going to come up here and help straighten things out," says Shay. "She wouldn't hear of it. Said she was a grownup and could handle Mac Albert herself. That's our Allie. After we hung up I called my boss at the marina, said my family had some problems and asked for a week off. He's a good guy and I've had no real time off since last winter, so he said okay. I grabbed some clothes, got in the car, stopped just for gas and burgers and coffee. Well, I had a couple of dozes alongside the road. I thought Allie might be back here by now. When that gal makes up her mind to do something, she don't let any grass grow under her feet. Runs in the family, I reckon." He grinned. "I'm gonna call her, then head up there and see what I can do to help with Mac and with her moving." Shay stands up.

"You looka here, now," says Pap. "You need some sleep before you go. Call her, by all means, but you don't need another two hours behind the wheel right now. May have to wait for the phone line, this time of day on Saturday. Come on, Billy Boy, let's you and me go out on the porch so your uncle can talk to your mama in private. And Punchy needs some yard time."

There's no one else on the line, so Shay dials the number, lets it ring eight times but there's no answer. "She's not there," he yells to Grandpap. "I'll get that nap and try her later."

"Sleep in my room, Uncle Shay," Billy calls out.

When they hear Billy's bedroom door close, Pap lets Punchy out and then heads for his chair. His back is still giving him fits. Billy stretches out on the couch. "I'm sure glad Uncle Shay's here, Pap."

"You and me both, boy," says Pap.

CHAPTER FORTY-ONE

THEY'RE BACK

Autumn is sitting on the rail at the end of the long Gulf pier, with her legs downstretched so she can splash her feet in the cool water. Watching birds swoop up and down and sometimes come up with a fish. Watching people throw their lines out, hoping to hook one of those fishes for themselves. She feels useless. It's Saturday morning. She's been in the Deep South for a week and has accomplished nothing. It appears there isn't anything she can do until Summer decides to leave. Which depends on Gulf Breeze.

Earlier, he was talking about the sad condition of the Greenstuff and Summer seemed to be listening, but a couple of hours ago she suddenly threw a hissy fit. She did some swooping up and down, herself, and puffing blazing hot air.

"I'm tired of being badgered," she said. "I'm not going to leave, and you two can like it or lump it!" Then she blew a great blast of heat at both of them and whooshed off. Gulf Breeze hadn't bothered to call to her, let alone go with her. Now he's breezing around on the pier and the fishermen are talking about how nice it is to get some cool air.

Sol is almost halfway across the sky. Autumn isn't going to stay there, waiting for Summer to come back. "I'm going over to see about Punchy and the boy," she says to Gulf Breeze.

"I'll go with you."

"Don't you think you ought to find Summer?" she asks.

"She'll come back when she cools off." Gulf Breeze laughs at his joke.

Autumn isn't amused. "That's exactly the problem—she doesn't want to cool off and she doesn't want anybody or anything else to cool off, either. I thought she'd listen to you."

"She does. She just won't admit she's wrong. Yet."

Not ever, Autumn thinks to herself, but she doesn't want to say it out loud—that might make it too true.

"Anyway, let's not worry about Summer right now. Come on." Gulf Breeze takes her hand and they have a cool whoosh together from the end of the pier, over the water and the dunes and the sea grass. When they get to the Tree they slow down and make sure there's no old pickup around.

At the little house, there's a very dirty car in the driveway, parked behind Big Beulah. Summer is sitting on one of the rockers, slowly moving back and forth. Punchy is lying at her feet, panting. He wags his stumpy tail, but doesn't get up.

"Hey there," says Summer, all friendly again. "This car belongs to Billy's uncle. He drove for days to get here. He's going to see Billy's mother, but he's in Billy's bedroom asleep right now because he's totally worn out from all that driving. Honestly, these humans need to learn to whoosh." She takes a deep breath and lets out hot air. For a change, she doesn't aim it at Autumn.

Autumn kneels down by Punchy. He welcomes her with a yip, but doesn't stir from his spot.

"Punchy's an okay dog," says Summer. He looks up at her. "He likes me. He likes me a lot." Autumn feels a pang of jealousy.

"So what are Billy and Pap doing?" asks Gulf Breeze.

"They rested up, then washed the dishes and now Pap's out on the back porch and Billy's in there reading a book. They're waiting for the uncle to finish his nap."

All of a sudden, Punchy jumps up and runs to the porch steps. His ears are pointed forward. He growls. Then the Weatherlings hear it: the old clunker truck, coming down the gravel road. Punchy runs to the screen door, barks loud, and heads back to the steps.

Billy hears the truck. "Pap, they're back!" He goes into his bedroom and pulls at his uncle's arm. "Wake up Uncle Shay! It's Fat Man and Pimples! They're back!"

Everybody is on the porch when the truck stops in the road out front. The rocker is still rocking. "Stop that," Autumn tells Summer. "Get out of that chair." For once, Summer listens to her, and the Weatherlings sit on the side railing.

Three people get out of the truck on the passenger side. The driver's door is still tied shut. Billy can't believe his eyes. His mother is with Fat Man and Pimples. She's looking at Billy as she comes up the steps. He turns away, to stand by Pap. Allie stops. Then she sees Shay by the door.

"Shay, I told you not to come! But I'm so glad you did!" She runs to him and he gives her a bear hug.

"Hey there, little sister. Nothing could have stopped me. I was planning to head on up to Crowley as soon as I got some sleep here. When we talked before, you didn't say anything about coming to Pap's. And certainly not with these low lifes."

"Oh, Shay." She's determined not to cry. She whispers to him. "Mac came by right after you called and told me they were driving down here to see Pap this morning and I'd better come with them if I knew what was good for me. I thought so, too. Didn't like to ride with them, but my car's acting up and I couldn't trust it. Shay, seems like everything has gone to pieces."

He takes her hand and looks her in the eye. "It's okay, gal. We'll get it straightened out."

Allie turns back to Billy. He's watching her. No expression on his face. *Oh lord, how am I ever going to get him to forgive me,* she thinks.

Fat Man walks up the steps, straight to Pap, and hands him a piece of paper. "You owe us money, old man, and here's the bill.

Fifty dollars for the job and a hundred for my truck door and thirty for the chain saw, another thirty for gas and our time. That's two hundred and ten dollars. And we want it *now*." Pimples starts to say something, but Fat Man jabs him in the ribs. "You keep your mouth shut, Sport. I told you I'd handle this."

Pap looks at the piece of paper and laughs. "You crazy? First and foremost, you didn't do the job and now it's called off. And second, your whole truck ain't worth a hundred dollars. Yeah, I can see the door's messed up, but I don't know how that happened. You probably backed into a tree with it open while you two was stealing my boy's dog. We can ask the sheriff what he thinks about that, I reckon."

Fat Man gets red in the face. "Why, you old buzzard."

Pap glances at the paper and keeps on going. "Gas money, yeah, I'll pay you that. That's around 20 cents a gallon. Ten gallons, at the most, for that old clunker to make it to here and back up to Crowley two times, so that's two dollars for gas."

He continues. "What your time's worth, well that's a good question, ain't it? I'd say it ain't worth much. What do you make an hour at them odd jobs you pick up? Maybe fifty cents? How long's a round trip from Crowley to here and back? About four hours. You done it twice, so that'd be eight hours. Four dollars apiece for that. Add the gas money, it all comes to ten dollars. I believe I can just about scrape that up."

Fat Man shakes his head. "Ain't you forgettin' something? Today makes three trips down here."

Pimples decides he's just got to put his oar in, too. "And you sure as heck owe us for that chain saw we had to borrow. We know it's been layin' out there all rusted up from that storm. If nobody's stole it. We gonna have to pay our buddy for it. That thing's worth more than thirty dollars, I'd say."

"The saw's okay," says Billy. "I know where it is. It's not far from here."

Pap looks at him. "Well, go get it, boy." Billy starts down the steps.

Pimples grabs Billy's shoulder. "Hold on, kid. I'm going with you." He only gets down a step before Punchy growls and takes hold of his pants leg. Pimples kicks out with his other foot, but the little dog holds on.

"No, Punchy. Let go, Punchy," Billy says. Punchy lets go, but he stays right there, looking at Pimples and growling.

"You ain't going nowhere, Sport," says Pap. "Shay, you help Billy Boy. Chain saw's too heavy for him with that sore ankle."

Billy isn't leaving Pap and Mama alone with these two guys. "No sir, I don't need any help. It's in a sack so I can pull it. I'll be back in no time. Punchy, you stay here."

CHAPTER FORTY-TWO

PAYOFF

As it turns out, the only protection needed is from Mac Albert's mouth. He curses and hollers and threatens to bring in the cops if Pap doesn't pay him and Sport what they have coming to them. His face gets redder and redder. Punchy stays just out of kicking range and growls.

"What you two got coming to you is some jail time for stealing my boy's dog," Pap says.

"That was Sport took him, not me."

"It was your truck that drove off with him, Mac Albert, and you driving it. It was your cabin where Billy Boy found him."

"That's right, Mr. Burnette. I'm not the one took him," Sport whines. "You're the one took him, Mac. Said you needed a squirrel dog."

"You keep your mouth shut."

"No, I ain't going to. You got me into this whole goldarned mess, said you had to have help, said it'd be easy as pie. I said okay I'd help you, but it's you planned the whole thing and it's you made a mess of it and it's *you* owes *me* money."

Mac Albert gives Sport a push that sends him stumbling down the steps. "I told you to keep your mouth shut. Looks like I'm going to have to shut it for you." He starts after Sport.

Shay grabs Mac's arm. "Hold it, mister. We're not having any fights here. You two can sort things out somewhere else. You get over there to those chairs, both of you, and cool down. I'll get you some water. No more talking, not a word, until the boy gets back with the saw." He goes inside to get two glasses, dips water from the bucket and gives each man a glass. Everybody's quiet until Billy comes back, dragging the sack. Shay takes it from him, pulls out the chain saw.

"It's in good shape." he says, "Here, look at it. Looks fine to me. You can take that off your list, Mac. Along with the door. Nobody here tore your truck up. What was that you figured, Pap?"

"I figured two dollars for gas and eight for their time. Total of ten dollars. That's generous."

Mac spits off the side of the porch. "Generous, nothin'. You promised us fifty dollars for killing the old tree and we went to all that trouble, borrowed a chain saw, got the job started, and you was the one called it off. Plus, your kid here caused me to hurt my knee. And you figure a measly ten dollars. I figure you owe us at least the fifty."

"You better figure different," says Pap. "Tell you what, I'll make it fifteen dollars and that's it. I'm going to pay you off and you two are going to git. I don't want to see hide nor hair of either one of you around here again. If I do, I'm calling the sheriff."

Mac looks at Pap's eyes, looks at Shay's muscles. "You low down, lying, old geezer! Okay, make it twenty and hand it over right now. I want to be shed of you and this whole business."

Pap puts his hand in his pocket and feels around. "I have to go inside to get it." He starts for the door.

Shay stops him. "I got it right here, Pap." He pulls out his billfold, takes out two tens and hands one to each of the men. Mac grabs his and Sport's, too.

"Hey!" yells Sport.

Mac picks up the chain saw and heads for the truck. Sport is right behind him, grabbing at the money. Mac stuffs both tens into his shirt pocket. He shoves Sport hard and Sport lands on his back in the middle of the yard. The big man moves fast, despite his hurt knee. He takes out his key, throws the chain saw into the back of the truck, gets in the passenger door, locks it, and rolls up the window. The motor grinds as he gets it started. Sport jumps on the running board and pulls at the locked door.

"Find your own way back, Dummy!" yells Mac. The truck heads down the road. Sport is standing on the running board, holding the door handle. He manages to grab onto the back of the truck and pull himself over into it.

On the porch, everybody's watching the action. When the truck gets past the blackberry bushes, Allie and Shay look at each other and start laughing. Shay says, "They're going the wrong way. You think they'll stop in town and spend all that money?" Allie hugs Pap and he starts laughing. Billy watches from the steps, grinning, with Punchy at his side.

Pap and Shay collapse in the swing. Billy looks down at Punchy, then over at his mom. She stops laughing and tears come to her eyes. She goes over and hugs him, but he turns his head away.

CHAPTER FORTY-THREE

SUMMER DECIDES

The Weatherlings are back on the rail at the end of the Gulf pier on Saturday night. Luna is smiling down at them, surrounded by what Autumn thinks must be about a jillion stars. Gulf Breeze is keeping cool air stirring and they all have their feet downstretched to the water. Two old men are sitting on a bench, holding fishing poles. They aren't saying anything or catching anything. Autumn figures they don't care, that they just like to be here in all the pleasantness.

Gulf Breeze laughs. "Pap and Billy and Uncle Shay sure showed those two guys."

"I wish you'd stop going on and on about that." Summer blasts a big stream of hot air at him. *Actually*, Autumn thinks, *he hasn't been going on and on*. They had talked about it as they whooshed their way to the pier, but not one of them has said much since they arrived here, and that was quite a while ago.

When the old pickup took off down the road with Fat Man and Pimples yelling at each other, the Weatherlings had floated to the top of the little house and stayed there cheering until it was out of sight. Then they came back down to the porch, where Billy and his mom were standing. She was wiping at her face with her hands and Billy was looking at the floor. Pap and Uncle Shay were swinging, still laughing about the way the tree killers had turned against each other and how ridiculous they looked, making their getaway. The

Weatherlings settled themselves on the porch rail until everyone, even Punchy, went inside.

Now, hours later, at the pier, they've been watching Luna get bigger, seeing more and more stars come out, listening to the water lap against the pilings of the pier and wriggling their toes in it. Everything has been fine. Until Summer's new tantrum. Autumn doesn't know what brought *this* one on. She, herself, loves to hear Gulf Breeze talk. His voice makes her happy.

The three sit in silence for a few minutes, then Summer says, "It's too cool here." She pulls her feet up from the water.

"It's always cooler out here on the end of the pier at night." Gulf Breeze sounds as pleasant as ever. "We can whoosh to the dry sand if you want to. It stays hotter there."

"No, I mean here. Not the pier. *Here.* This whole place. The Deep South."

Autumn is amazed. Cool? Why, it's still hot as a blast furnace. She hasn't felt all-over, inside-out cool since she first landed on the top of her Tree.

Gulf Breeze looks out at the water and smiles. "We can't make it any hotter here than it already is, Summer. Sorry, but you've loved it up to now."

"It's been okay. It's been good compared to...well, to any place north of here. I thought it was as hot as anywhere could be until I heard Billy's uncle today, talking about where he lives. Did you catch the name of that place?"

"Key West," is the prompt answer. Autumn thinks it's a little too prompt. Like maybe Gulf Breeze has been waiting for that question.

"Key West. Right. He said it's way below the Deep South and it's always warm there. Always. And if it's so much farther south, it's got be warmer than here. I'd like to see it. I might like to live there. Do you know exactly where it is? Can you take me to Key West?"

"I know where it is, sure," says Gulf Breeze. "All the way down at the end of Florida. When would you want to go?"

"Tomorrow," says Summer. "Let's go tomorrow."

Autumn feels a delicious shiver. Summer *wanting* to leave! Could it be true?

"I can't leave that soon," says Gulf Breeze. I've got things to do here before I go skydoodling off. Lots of things. But I ought to be able to get away in...I'd say...maybe in a month. For a few days."

Autumn's heart sinks.

Summer frowns at Gulf Breeze. "A month is too long. I'm not going to hang around here when there's some place hotter. You've been telling me I ought to leave because of the Greenstuff, so you can just help me do it."

He smiles at her. "You don't need me to take you." Both Summer and Autumn look at him. "I know how you can hitch a ride," he says.

It takes Summer a moment, then she understands. "Uncle Shay," she says. "He'll be going back down there Monday. Uncle Shay. Sure, I can wait two days." She thinks about it. "But I want you to come, too, Breeze Buddy."

"Can't do it Summer. Not now. I'll visit later on."

"You sure?" Summer looks skeptical.

"I'm sure. Maybe Autumn will come, too."

Summer looks over at Autumn. "I didn't ask her," she says. Autumn feels a pang. She thought Summer had come to like her, at least a little bit. She turns away from both of them.

"Anyway, she has to hang around here, do her cool thing. Right, Miss Butinsky?" Summer gives Autumn's back a little push. Autumn turns around, ready to tell Summer just what she thinks of her. Then she sees the smile on Summer's face. Gulf Breeze is grinning.

"Actually," Summer says, "we're quite a threesome. We oughta call ourselves The Good Deeds Weatherling Trio."

Gulf Breeze laughs. "We could shorten it to the Goody-We-Three."

"How about," says Autumn, "the Rocking Weatherlings?"

CHAPTER FORTY-FOUR

BILLY IS WORRIED

Billy's brain won't turn off when he goes to bed Saturday night. So much to think about. Uncle Shay wanting to take him and Pap and Mama and Punchy down to Key West to live. Mama excited about it and ready to pick up and go right away. Pap saying it might be a good thing for them, but no, this has been his home nigh on to 70 years and he ain't planning on living anywhere else. Uncle Shay saying Mama wouldn't have any trouble finding a waitressing job, and she and Billy could stay with him until she finds an apartment. Saying that Billy would love living on that key jutting out into the ocean. Billy didn't have anything to say, himself. And then Mama and Uncle Shay took off for Crowley right after supper, to see to everything there. Saying they'd be back Monday morning to get Billy and Punchy. Billy was glad when they left. He'd thought about running down to talk to Rick, but his grandpap got so quiet, Billy didn't want to leave him.

Punchy's awake, too. He whines. "Come on up here, fella," says Billy. Stroking his little dog calms both of them.

When Billy wakes up Sunday morning, he thinks about what Mama said. She's going to rent out her house furnished. She won't hear of selling it. She'll have to write notes to the electric company and the phone company. And call the paperboy. She'll drop off a note with a "For Rent" ad at the newspaper office. She has to pack her clothes. Shay will help her clean the house. They'll get some rest, too, and on Monday they'll come down as early as they can to pick up Billy and Punchy. She's going to leave her car in Crowley; Uncle Shay says he thinks it needs too much work. Anyway, it's a mighty long trip on that two-lane road and Shay's planning for them to drive straight through, so they'll trade off driving and sleeping. He needs to be back to work at the marina on Thursday, for sure.

Billy hasn't forgiven Mama. He knows he should, but he hasn't. He's forgiven Grandpap for wanting to do something to get the money they need, but he hasn't forgiven her for bringing in Fat Man and Pimples. He doesn't think he'll ever be able to. If he hadn't run into Annette up there at Catfish Cabins, he doesn't know what he'd have done to get Punchy back. Thinking about Annette gets his mind on happier things. He's told Mama about Annette and her dad wanting to find a place with enough land for a garden and that maybe they'll want to rent Mama's house. She's going to get in touch with Mr. Powers. Maybe Mr. Powers can even sell Mama's car for her. Somebody at the lumber mill might buy it and get it fixed up.

Annette Powers. He hopes he'll see her again. That makes him think about Rick. What in the world is he going to do without Rick? What will Rick do without him? Those dang Randalls will make Rick's life miserable without that hunting trip to look forward to.

And what about Pap? How's he going to get along? Billy tries to shove that out of his mind, but it shoves right back in. And every time he thinks about Pap, there's Grandmam right behind Pap, looking at Billy with her bright blue eyes, smiling and waiting. But Billy doesn't know what she's waiting for. He wishes she'd say something. He looks down at his wristband and thinks *what would Daddy say?*

GOODBYES ARE HARD

"**P**ap, it's almost two o'clock. The Showers oughta be back from church and finished eating by now. I got to go see Rick." Billy has washed and dried the Sunday breakfast and lunch dishes. He wipes water off the little counter and hangs the cloth on its hook over the sink. "He doesn't even know I'm leaving."

"Sure, boy, you run on. Spend the rest of the day with him, if it's okay with his folks."

Pap is tired. He's been thinking he needs to look around to see what else he can find to give his grandson to take to Florida. They'd pulled Sally's old suitcase from under Pap's bed last night and dusted it off, so there's something to take clothes in. Most of them are dirty. He told Allie about that, before she left with Shay, but she said it didn't matter, she'd take care of the washing in Florida. Pap would wash them, himself, but he doesn't feel up to it. His back is hurting worse than ever.

Punchy's at the front door. Billy opens it and the little dog runs out, down the steps and onto the driveway. He stops and looks back, like he's wondering why Billy is so slow.

"Hold on a minute, Punch, I got to get something." Billy goes under the front porch and comes out with the makeshift crutch Rick rigged for him after the fight at the Tree. He waves it in the air as he and Punchy run down the road. His ankle's a whole lot better.

Billy's been thinking he'll wait until they're alone to tell Rick about leaving, but it doesn't work out that way. Rick and his parents already know there's been a visitor from Florida. Somebody saw the car and told them. Mr. and Miz Showers try not to sound nosy, but when he says it was his Uncle Shay, they have all sorts of questions. The next thing he knows, he's told them about the plan to move to Key West and they're saying how Rick is going to miss him and how they're going to miss him, and what in the world will his granddaddy do without him but isn't it exciting and he's going to love Florida, they just know. Rick isn't saying anything.

In a few minutes, Miz Showers looks at the boys and gets quiet. When Mr. Showers starts to ask something else, she shushes him. "We can't sit here gabbing all day, Frank. And I expect these boys have some things to talk about. We'll take care of your chores, Rick. And Billy, you stay for supper." She shoos them out onto the front porch.

"You want to go down to the Tree, Billy?" Rick doesn't look at his friend.

"No, let's just sit here on the swing and cool off." They swing back and forth, not saying anything for a while. Punchy lies nearby with his muzzle on his paws, watching them.

"I sure am glad you got Punchy back," says Rick. "He's one smart dog, aren't you, boy?" He stops the swing and bends over to scratch the little dog's head.

"How long you think you'll live in Florida?" He sits back and starts the swing moving again with his foot.

"Supposed to live down there from now on." Billy helps keep the movement going, back and forth, back and forth.

"Maybe your mama won't like it and you'll move back. Anyway, you'll come home to see your grandpap."

"Mama says we'll come visit, but not for a while. We have to get settled. She has to find a job. As soon as she does that, and rents out the house in Crowley, she wants us to get our own place. Uncle Shay's only got one bedroom and a couch."

"Where you going to sleep?"

"Dang if I know. Uncle Shay just said he'd make room for us, didn't say how he'd do it. Maybe give Mama the bed, take the couch himself, make me a pallet on the floor." Billy doesn't want to talk about it anymore. "Hey, Rick, I brought you something." He stops the swing and gets up to retrieve the makeshift crutch from where he had laid it by the porch steps. When he hands it to Rick, he grins.

Rick grins back. "We sure showed those guys, didn't we, buddy? Old Fat Man and Pimples. They won't be coming back."

Billy's grin gets broader. He's been saving this to tell his buddy, not much wanting Mr. and Miz. Showers to know what all had happened. "They did come back. Drove up yesterday in that old pickup, with the door tied closed, Fat Man limping with his hurt knee and mouthing off, demanding their pay. Wanted two hundred and ten dollars, Rick. Two hundred and ten dollars!"

"Oh, man! No kidding! What happened? Did your grandpap pay them?"

"Shoot, no!" Billy tells how Pap and Uncle Shay handled the tree cutters, and how Uncle Shay gave them each just ten dollars, and how the big man took all the money. It gets funnier and funnier. By the time he gets to the last part, where Fat Man drives off with Pimples scrambling to get on the back of the truck, the two boys are jumping around, laughing and shadow boxing. Punchy's jumping right along with them, barking like crazy.

They spend the rest of the afternoon pitching prickle pods, throwing sticks for Punchy to chase after, and swinging on the porch when they get too hot. For supper, Rick's mama has ham loaf and carrot salad and green beans and lemon meringue pie and big cloverleaf yeast rolls. All left over from Sunday dinner. Billy eats until he's stuffed. But he starts thinking about Pap alone in the house, maybe eating, maybe not, sadder and sadder. Getting into that bottle in the cupboard. He also thinks about his Tree. He's got to say goodbye to it. As soon as everyone's finished eating, he gets up from the table and thanks Miz Showers.

"I'd better get on," he says. "There's things to do and Pap's back is real bad." Rick goes with him out to the porch.

"I'll send you a postcard when I get to Florida, Rick. Uncle Shay used to send us postcards sometimes. Maybe your folks'll bring you down there for a vacation. Uncle Shay says people come from all over the country."

"I'll ask them about it." Rick doesn't hold out a whole lot of hope. Neither does Billy.

"I'll see you." Billy starts up the road.

Punchy stays, looking at Rick.

"Go on, fellow." Rick pats the little dog on his head, picks up the stick crutch, and as he goes inside he hears Billy yell:

"I'm gonna get us two gator knives, Rick!"

CHAPTER FORTY-SIX

BAD TIME

By the time Billy and Punchy get home, it's dark and Pap is sitting on his porch rocker with a pillow stuffed behind his back. Billy comes up the steps slowly. He's got his slingshot and rocks in one pants pocket, arrowheads in another, sea shells in both hands. Two pot lids are tucked under his right arm. He lines everything up on the porch rail, by the water bucket.

"Well, you been gone awhile, boy. You and Rick had a lot to talk about, I reckon. You need a snack?"

"Thanks, Pap, I ain't hungry. Miz Showers had a big supper. Me and Punchy weren't there all this time, though; we came back by the Tree."

"You get your goodbyes said to it?"

Billy sits down in Grandmam's rocker. "No sir. I couldn't do it."

Pap stops rocking. "Well, I see you cleared out the hole; what else did you do down there?" He doesn't say anything about the pot lids.

"I checked on the gash. It's better already. I looked at yours and Grandmam's heart. And I climbed all the way to the top. It was so quiet, I stayed a while, thinking about things. Sorry we're so late."

"No, no, that's all right. I expect you needed some time to yourself after all that's happened. And going to happen."

"Yeah, Pap, that's what I was thinking about. I thought about Grandmam, too. I hate to go off and leave her."

"Aw, Billy, you ain't leaving Grandmam. You'll remember her no matter where you go. You'll take her with you. Your daddy, too. And me." Pap clears his throat, gets up, leans over to stretch his back, and heads to the door. "You two come on in pretty quick. You and me need to decide for sure what all you're taking." He goes inside without looking back.

The swing starts swinging and Grandpap's rocker starts rocking. Punchy runs to the chair and barks. "Hey there, Punchy. Good to see you." Autumn laughs, remembering how Summer had called him Pokey before, and swings harder.

"Watch out," says Gulf Breeze. "The boy is going to suspect something."

"Billy knows," says Autumn. "He already thanked me for what you did at the tree. He thinks I did it and I had no way to tell him different. We need to show him that there's three of us."

"Looks like our Tree friend is back, Punch," says Billy. "Hey, looks like there's more than one!" He gets out of Grandmam's chair, stills it and watches. It starts rocking by itself. "Two rockers and the swing all moving. There must be at least three!" If only he could see what Punchy sees. He wants to tell Pap about the Tree Friends, but thinks better of it. He could have told Grandmam. He couldn't tell his mother. He shrugs. "Come on, Punchy," he says. "I got to get you cleaned up before you can go to Florida."

"Yes, go on, Punchy," says Autumn. "We'll see you in the morning before you go."

Punchy barks at the Weatherlings before he follows Billy. Billy looks back at the rockers and the swing and waves. "Thanks again. To *all* of you!"

Autumn is delighted. "See? He knows!"

"Yes, he does. He's a smart boy." Gulf Breeze is smiling.

Summer is smiling, too. "And Punchy's a smart dog. I'll look after him in Florida."

Autumn looks at her, saying nothing, but thinking that Punchy is her particular friend and she doesn't like Summer horning in. Autumn's going to miss Punchy. But, then she thinks maybe it's good that a Rocking Weatherling will be down there with him, making sure he's okay. Even if it has to be Miss Know-it-All.

So all she says is, "Thanks, Summer."

The three settle back to their rocking and swinging and end up staying all night.

Billy is still awake at two a.m. When he and Punchy went to bed, Pap settled into his chair with a drink from his bottle, and now Billy can hear him snoring. Punchy is making little dream whimpers on the foot of the bed. Billy gets up and goes to the window. He thinks about Pap and traces the initials on his wrist band. Over and over.

CHAPTER FORTY-SEVEN

TIME TO LEAVE

"Wake up, boy." Pap is patting Billy on his shoulder. "It's Monday already. Shay said they'd be here early as they can and it's 8:30 now. You get yourself a good bath while I start breakfast."

Billy opens his eyes, looks at Pap, remembers. He closes his eyes for a minute, then sits up in bed. "I can't do it, Pap," he says.

"You got to have a bath, boy. I ain't sending you off to Florida dirty. Come on now, get moving."

"I'm not talking about a bath."

Pap looks at him. "Well, what in tarnation *are* you talking about?"

"I mean I'm not going."

Pap thinks about that for a moment. Then he shakes his head. "Your mama says you're going. Your mama wants you to go. It's her say-so. It's not yours and it's not mine, Billy Boy."

"Pap, I'd just be a worry to her down there. She has to think about getting a job and a place to live; she don't need to be worrying about me. Anyhow, I don't want to go. I want to stay with you. And I don't want to leave Rick. I won't know a single soul down there."

Pap understands what Billy is saying. He also knows that Billy has mixed feelings about his mother. But he can't let on to his grandson that he agrees. He wants to. He wants to say yes, all that's pretty much true. He wants to say he doesn't know what he'll do without him. But he can't say that. He can't come between the boy

159

and his mother. So what he says is, "You'll have your mama and your uncle there. And you'll have Punchy. And you'll get started in school and make friends."

Billy's jaw is set. "I'm not going." He looks around. "Where's Punchy?"

"He hightailed it for the front porch as soon as I opened your door. Seemed like he was just waiting to get out. Didn't even try to get you up. Knows something's going on, I reckon. You come on now, get your bath. As for going or not going, you'll have to talk to your mother about that. But she wants you to go. And I tell you, she's got the say in this."

Billy gets up and checks on Punchy, but the little dog doesn't want to come in from the porch. *The Tree Friends must still be here,* Billy thinks, as he goes into the bathroom. When he comes out to the kitchen, clean and dressed, Pap is frying sausage and eggs, and Uncle Shay's car is pulling up in the driveway. Billy goes to meet them.

Allie gets out of the car and hugs Billy. "Hey there. You ready for the big adventure?" He tolerates the hug, but draws away as they walk up the steps. He looks at Uncle Shay, who looks back at him like he's trying to figure out what Billy is thinking.

Punchy is sitting by the swing. He runs to the steps to bark a welcome. Then he runs to Grandmam's rocker, over to Grandpap's, and back to the swing, where he stands wriggling and yipping.

"My goodness, Punchy, you're antsy this morning." Allie laughs at him. "You nervous about this trip? Or just saying goodbye to the porch?" She's glad to focus on the little dog instead of her son. Autumn, Summer and Gulf Breeze vacate the chairs and swing, and whoosh onto the roof.

"Punchy, stop looking at us," says Autumn. "We don't want the others to know we're here."

Billy is the only one who notices that the rockers and swing suddenly jerk, sway a little, then get still. "They're here," he says to himself.

"What did you say, honey?"

"Nothing, Mama."

She looks at him closely. He's sure making it plain he's not happy. Well, that's natural, leaving home and all. The only home he remembers. *But he'll adjust*, she tells herself. *He'll get used to it. And used to me and I'll be a better mama to him now.*

Pap has cooked a fine breakfast. Sausage and eggs, grits and biscuits and Miz Garraway's fig preserves. Uncle Shay says he hasn't had breakfasts as good as Pap's since he moved to Florida. Then he thinks better of it because he doesn't want to say anything that will make Billy think Key West isn't a fine place, so he says that well, there are a couple of cafes where the cooking is almost this good and there's a drug store with a superdooper soda fountain.

Billy isn't paying any attention to what Uncle Shay says, anyway. He's having too much trouble trying to eat, what with his stomach all knotted up. He sees Pap watching him, waiting for him to say something. But it's hard to get the words started. Then they're all finished and getting up from the table and saying how stuffed they are and thanking Pap.

"You get your teeth brushed," says Allie. "We'll take your stuff out to the car. You got everything gathered up?"

Billy knows he's run out of time and he blurts it out. "Mama, I'm not going."

Allie looks at him. "What are you talking about? Of course you're going." Her voice is impatient.

"I can't go, Mama. I'm sorry." He looks down at his feet.

Pap claps Uncle Shay on the shoulder. "Let's you and me go on out to the porch, Shay. Looks like these two need to have a little talk." As the men leave the front room, Allie takes Billy's hand and leads him to the sofa. Punchy lays down in front of them, looking back and forth from one to the other.

Allie takes a deep breath and gets her voice under control. "Okay, tell me what you're thinking, Billy," she says. So Billy does.

CHAPTER FORTY-EIGHT

OFF TO FLORIDA

Allie starts crying as soon as the car is out of sight of Pap's house.

Summer, in the back seat, is disappointed that Billy and Punchy aren't with them. She doesn't know why they aren't.

Earlier, the Weatherlings were enjoying rocking and swinging when Pap and Uncle Shay came out and sat on the porch steps. Summer got up to go inside and see what Billy and his mother and Punchy were doing, but Autumn said "Oh, for Nature's sake, Summer, leave them alone."

Summer was surprised. Autumn had never spoken that sharply to her before. *Well, Miss-Do-Everything-Mama-N-Says,* she thought. *I'm glad to see you have a little spunk.* But she shrugged like she didn't care and moved to the swing with Gulf Breeze. The three in the front room finally came out. Billy hugged his mother and his uncle. He and Punchy didn't go with them to the car. Pap went down the steps, hugged Allie, shook hands with Shay, then came back to stand by Billy.

When the car started, Summer was still on the swing, wondering what was happening. Gulf Breeze had to give her a little push. "Go on, Summer. You'll get left." She whooshed herself through the back window as the car drove off, everybody waving and calling goodbye, including Autumn and Gulf Breeze.

Now Summer's sitting in the back seat, looking out the window. On her way to Key West! She hopes Allie quits that blubbering soon.

Shay lets Allie cry herself out. Then he asks, "So what happened? What did Billy say?"

"He said he couldn't leave Pap. That Pap needs him. And that it would be harder for me if he was to come along."

"What did you say?"

"I told him I love him and *I* need him, too. And that I've always wanted him to live with me but I just couldn't handle everything before. That now I can do better. I can get a good job and make a home for him.

"But you know, Shay, I have to admit that he's probably right. I need to get settled, need to make some money, need to get more education so I can get a better job. I need to be able to give him a decent home. I can't do that yet, I know I can't. And I need to learn to control my temper, be more patient with him. Anyway, his mind was all made up and I finally had to say okay. You think I was right, Shay?"

"What I think is, if he knows you love him and you really wanted him to come with you, well, Allie, that's what he needs to know right now."

"He said he knows it. When I hugged him, he hugged me back. I guess he loves me. But he loves his grandpap more, and to tell the truth, I don't know how Pap *could* do without him." She starts crying again. "Billy's so much like his daddy, Shay. I'm proud of him. I wish I was a better mother."

Shay reaches over and pats her arm. "I'm proud of both of you, Sis."

Well that explains that, Summer thinks. *And there she goes, blubbering again. Whatever. All I care about is we're heading far, far south, where it never, never gets cold.* She stretches and settles herself into the back seat for a nice, long, hot trip.

I can do without the boy, she thinks. *But when he comes to visit I hope he brings Punchy.*

CHAPTER FORTY-NINE

BILLY AND PAP

When the car heads off for Florida, Billy and Pap go back to the kitchen. "It's too late to go to school, Pap. I'd better get on to washing these dishes. There's sure a lot of them. That was some breakfast." Billy starts stacking up plates from the table. He feels like if he doesn't do something, he may cry. Watching his mother and Uncle Shay drive off had been harder than he had expected.

"Naw, boy, you need to put your things away. Then you and Punchy go on outside, take the day off. I'll do what needs to be done in here. My old back's feeling a whole lot better this morning." He takes hold of Billy's shoulders and steers him into the living room, where the suitcase is sitting.

Billy hesitates, looks at his grandpap, then over at the corner cupboard. "I'd rather hang around. I'm kind of tired."

Pap sees the look. "You don't need to worry none about me, boy. Go on now. Do as I say."

It doesn't take much time to get unpacked. Billy drags it out as long as he can. He divides his dirty clothes into two piles, light and dark, and adds Pap's to them. He even gets the broom and dust pan and sweeps under Pap's bed before he puts the suitcase back. He's thinking about that bottle. Pap is mighty happy that he's staying and might think that's a cause for celebrating. Punchy, on the other hand, is raring to go. He keeps racing back and forth between Billy, wherever Billy happens to be, and the screen door.

"Hold your horses, Punchy." Billy laughs, partly at Punchy, but mostly because he's happy to be home and not on his way to Florida.

He finally runs out of things to do. His grandpap is finished in the kitchen and has gone out on the back porch. He's sitting there with his coffee mug, looking up at the clear blue sky. When Billy joins him, Pap stretches a hand up in the air.

"Not a sign of a breeze, boy, but it's not quite as hot. We need us a lot of rain and we need us some cool weather. This heat and drought has parched everything. How about if you and Punchy get on down to that tree and do a rain dance or something." He looks at Billy and grins. "I'm glad you stayed, Bill."

Bill! Billy's face lights up. "I'm glad, too, Pap."

He starts to go into the house, but turns back. He grabs hold of his wrist band and says, "Pap, there's one thing I want to talk to you about." He hesitates. Pap waits. "It's about that bottle. I..."

"That's enough, boy. I don't need no lectures from you." Pap's voice is gruff. "You go on down and see your tree."

Billy turns and as he goes in the back door he says, in a low voice, "I love you, Pap."

Pap doesn't turn to look at Billy and doesn't say anything back. But he brushes at his eyes, then acts like he's swiping at a bug. Billy goes through the house to the front porch where Punchy is stretched out, watching the swing sway back and forth. Grandpap's chair is rocking, too.

"Our Tree Friends are here again, Punch." He waves at the swing and rocker. "I wish I could see them like you can." He thinks about his friend that he *can* see: Rick. Billy can't tell Rick the good news, because he's at school, but he's just bustin' to tell somebody. "Hey, Punch, you and me are going down and let Rick's folks know we're staying here. Then we'll tell the Tree." He laughs and unbuttons his shirt. "Let's go. Race you. Race *all* of you. Come on!" He motions to the swing and rocker as he and Punchy take off.

"Let's go with them," says Autumn.

"You go on. I've got things to do," Gulf Breeze says. "And you need to get busy pretty soon, yourself. I'll meet you at the Underpier later." He whooshes himself away and Autumn heads for the Showers' house with Billy and Punchy.

Pap gets up from his chair on the back porch and stretches. His back is feeling pretty darn good. Like a big weight's off it. He goes inside, carrying his empty mug, and heads straight for the corner cupboard. He takes the bottle into the kitchen, opens it, and pours the whiskey down the sink.

CHAPTER FIFTY

READY TO WORK

It's Tuesday morning and Autumn is sitting at the top of the Tree. When she returned to it the night before, it welcomed her with happy rustles, just like always. The leaves arranged themselves to make her canopied bed, and she slept soundly. Now Sol is well up in the blue, blue sky. Autumn is so comfortable she doesn't want to move, but it's time to get to work. With Summer gone to Florida, it's already cooler in the Deep South, but there's still much to do. Gulf Breeze will be along soon.

She upstretches to look around and thinks about all the things that have happened since she arrived. That was twelve days ago! She sure has a lot more confidence now. She knows the territory and, though her training was short and not what anyone would call complete, Mother Nature did teach her a lot of things. Now that she's been able to relax, she's remembering more and more of them. She has also learned a lot from Gulf Breeze and, she has to admit, from Summer, too.

Opinionated, stubborn Summer. Autumn smiles. How will her hot-headed Weatherling friend fare down there at the tip of Florida on that little key? She wishes Summer well, but she's so relieved to be rid of her. It will be good to get a lovely, cool, colorful fall started. Autumn hears a rustling of leaves at the bottom of the Tree, then three barks.

Punchy has come to help.

THANK YOU TO
THE PRICKLE POD SQUAD

All the Slaters:
Carl, Keith, Derek, Mary Ellen, Kate, Elizabeth, Jesse, Ky

Susan Martinello, Mary Ardis, Sonya Bennett,
Sue Brannan Walker, Mickey Cleverdon, Elsie Pritchard,
Steve Bostic, and Bert Johnston.

John O'Melveny Woods, Jessica Trippe, and David Philips

ABOUT THE AUTHOR

Glenda Richmond Slater grew up in the Deep South climbing magnolia trees, swimming in the Gulf of Mexico, and discovering lost lanes. She's the author of *The Junk Food King* and *Fooling Around with Shakespeare*, and lives in Spanish Fort, Alabama, where she writes fiction and poetry for all ages.